COWBOY FOUND

KINGS OF MONTANA, BOOK 3

VANESSA GRAY BARTAL

DRY CREEK PRESS

CHAPTER 1

*I*sabelle Landry was thinking about hair dryers. Specifically, she was thinking of the universality of hair dryers. Whether in her rural hometown beauty shop or the chic Manhattan salon where she now sat, there were always hair dryers. Realizing how much time she had just spent thinking about an inanimate object, she searched around for something to entertain herself while she waited for her new golden highlights to set.

A magazine was out of reach. Stretching her arm as long as she could, she barely grazed the magazine with her fingertips and began inching it toward her body. At last, it was within grasp. She pulled it close and saw it was already opened. She started to close it and stopped. The picture at the top of the page was achingly familiar, a prairie landscape with a lone mountain in the background. For that reason, she began reading the fictional short story instead of flipping to the fluffy advice column, as was her first inclination.

By the time her stylist, Jeff, came to retrieve her, her shoulders were shaking with silent tears and her mascara ran in rivers down her cheeks. He peered over her shoulder to see what was causing her to cry.

"Oh, I see you've found the story," he said when he turned off her dryer. "You're the fifth person today who has cried over that thing."

"This is magical. It's amazing." She hugged the magazine to her chest. "Do you mind if I take this with me? I'll pay you."

Jeff waved his hand dismissively. "Please, honey, I would be glad to get rid of it. I'm sick of all the tears that thing has caused in here lately. No offense."

"None taken." She sniffled and smiled appreciatively at him when he handed her a tissue. As he finished styling her hair, she finished the story and greedily scanned the author's bio at the bottom of the page. And then she gasped so hard she choked and coughed.

"What now?" Jeff asked.

She tapped the magazine. "This writer is from my hometown."

He gave her a look that seemed to say, *So what's the big deal?*

"You don't understand," she continued, tapping the page imperiously. "I'm from the middle of nowhere Montana. There are four thousand people in the entire town, and none of them have the ability to write like this."

"Things change," Jeff said.

"Not in Montana. Not like this." She pressed her lips together, excitement buzzing in her ears.

"So what are you going to do about it?" Jeff asked. It was strange her stylist knew her so well, but the old adage was true; she had told this man her life story on more than one occasion, and he had been her stylist for four years. By now, he knew her as well as anyone.

"I'm going to go to Montana. I'm going to find this woman, and I'm going to make a million dollars." She started to get out of the chair, but he pulled her back.

"Not until I'm finished perfecting your hair. Sit still," he commanded.

Meekly, she sat back and obeyed. Jeff had worked a miracle in her, and for that reason she was under his complete authority. She wanted to tell him to hurry so she could get back to her office, but she didn't dare. Instead, she sat still and silent, trying not to squirm impatiently in her seat until at last he was finished. And as she inspected herself in the giant mirror, she had to admit it had been worth the wait.

"You're a genius and I love you," she told him.

"I know. Don't forget me and stay in Podunk, Montana," he admonished.

She snorted indelicately. "No chance of that. I worked my tail off to get out of there. I will never live there again."

Jeff cocked an eyebrow at her. "Careful what you say you'll never do, darling, or you'll find yourself doing exactly that."

She shivered, trying not to let his words get to her. There was no way she would ever consider going back to Montana on a permanent basis. She would rather die. If not for the story in her hands, she wouldn't even consider going back there temporarily. But the story was too good, and she had a feeling about it. It was the same feeling that, a year ago, had propelled her to fight for an author whose manuscript she pulled out of the slush pile. At that time, she had been a secretary at the fledgling literary agency where she had worked all through college. The true literary agents were overworked and had found amusement in Isabelle's excitement over manuscripts they deemed as little more than birdcage liners. No one expected her to find anything worthwhile in the pile of papers waiting to go to the shredder. And, at first, no one had listened to her when she said she had found something special. After all, she was a secretary, new to the field, and barely out of college. What did a twenty one year old kid know about literature?

A lot, as it turned out. With her usual indomitable perseverance, Isabelle had fought for the right to represent the author. She insisted she would continue her secretarial duties while she tried to find a publisher for the unknown author in her spare time. Since the agency had nothing to lose and since they were tired of hearing her talk about it, they capitulated. And then quickly realized it was the best decision they ever made. Within two weeks, Isabelle had arranged a bidding war between three of the largest publishers in the industry. Her client's book quickly shot to number one on the bestseller list and stayed there for three months, earning the writer, the publisher,

Isabelle, and her entire company a large sum of money and a whole lot of prestige. For that reason, she had switched from a secretary to the agency's top literary agent almost overnight and now had people pounding down her door to represent them. In addition to her bull-dog, take-no-prisoner's negotiation strategy, she had a reputation as having a keen sense about new writers.

That was why when she let herself into her boss's office with a twinkle of excitement in her eyes, her boss picked up her phone, told her secretary to hold her calls, and leaned forward anxiously.

"What have you got, Belle?" Nancy Jarvis asked with barely masked excitement.

"I found something," Belle said. "This." She held out the magazine for the other woman to see. Knowing Nancy's time was limited, she summarized for her. "It's a short story written by an unknown. I checked. No one is representing the author. No one has even heard of her."

"And you want to represent her," Nancy surmised. "Sounds great."

"It's not so simple," Belle said. "When I say the author is unknown, I mean she's really unknown. She's using a pseudonym. Furthermore, she's from my hometown in Montana. The people out there are... indescribable. The point is, I'm going to have to finesse this one in person."

"Why?" Nancy asked.

"Because knowing the people there the way I do, whoever this is probably doesn't want to be published. They like their solitude and anonymity. I have the feeling I'm going to have to do some convincing."

"What do you need?" Nancy asked, already willing to do whatever it took to get the author. If Belle said she was worth it, Nancy would bend over backwards to get a contract. She might be young, but Belle Landry had immense drive, talent, and instincts. Already she had made the company enormous amounts of money and found four authors, all of whom were currently on the bestseller list. And unlike some shining stars Nancy had worked with in the past, Belle wasn't cocky, didn't try to step on anyone to feather her own nest. She merely wanted to do her best, something she had accomplished completely, at least so far.

"I need two weeks off to go to Montana. I need to find this girl and convince her in person to sign with me."

"Two weeks," Nancy said, blowing out a breath. There was never enough time in Manhattan, especially not in their industry. Two weeks here was like a year everywhere else. But she trusted Belle. Rarely had she seen someone with so much drive and enthusiasm for the job. If she said this was what she needed to get the contract, then this was what she needed. "All right. Go. But try to get it done in less than two weeks and hurry back."

"Believe me, I want to get this over with as soon as possible so I can return to civilization. I'm not sure I can go two weeks without Thai food." They shared a smile and Belle returned to her office. Anticipating Nancy's answer would be affirmative, she had already assigned a private detective to track down the author's mailing address. To her delight, when she finished booking her flight she received a message from the detective.

With nervous fingers, she clicked open her email and scanned the address, reading it twice to make sure she hadn't misread it. She knew the address by heart, of course. She had known the family all her life. But she was also sure there had to be some mistake. The author absolutely, positively could not live where the address said she lived.

She sat back and crossed her arms over her chest, fighting down a sudden jolt of anxiety. "Get ready, King brothers, Belle Landry is coming home," she whispered. Then she picked up the phone and called her mom.

CHAPTER 2

*B*elle was unprepared for the tidal wave of emotion her journey home would produce. She had left willingly, happily, when she was seventeen years old, and she had never looked back. In the last four years, she hadn't been back to visit once, much to her mother's irritation. Belle had put her off by telling her she didn't have the money for a flight. And, while up until a year ago that had been true, it wasn't the real reason she hadn't returned. The truth was Belle and Montana had never been a good fit. Bookish and ambitious, she hadn't liked cows, horses, or sports.

For her high school graduation, she asked her parents for an airplane ticket to New York. Reluctantly, they agreed. And so she had left home with a hundred dollars in her pocket and all her worldly possessions in a battered suitcase from Goodwill. And somehow she had made it—not that there had been much doubt she would. She was and had always been a bulldozer. When she set her mind to something, she did it. For as long as she could remember, she had wanted to be a literary agent. When she landed in New York, the first place she went was to the agency where she now worked. She insisted on seeing the person in charge, told him she wanted to be an agent, and asked for a corner office. Amused by her plucky attitude, he hired her as a secretary to his secretary. He also recommended an apartment for her with his daughter who was a student at NYU.

Belle and his daughter, Ruth, had hit it off right away and roomed together in a tiny one room walkup for four years until Ruth graduated NYU and Belle graduated from the community college where she attended night school. And then last year Belle had hit the mother lode with her author and could finally afford to live in an apartment with a bedroom and a doorman. Ruth married a man from the middle of nowhere Indiana and now lived there and taught high school art.

Her phone rang, startling her out of her reverie. She picked it up from the seat beside her, noting as she did that she kept her eyes on the road—a habit she had picked up in New York. In Montana, there was so little traffic she could probably read *War and Peace* and still keep her car on the road. In Manhattan, she had to watch traffic every second to keep from colliding with another vehicle.

"Hello," she said absently, her mind so far away she hadn't checked the caller ID.

"This is me, returning your call." It was her boyfriend, Storm. "Are we on for tonight?"

Her gaze fell on the road sign telling her she was thirty minutes from her hometown. "Uh, no. I'm not going to be able to make it. I'm in Montana."

"Who died?"

She gave a nervous chuckle. "No one. I'm working."

"Oh. When will you be back?"

"Two weeks."

"Two weeks? What am I supposed to do alone for the next two weeks?"

"You could fly out here and visit. My parents are curious about you."

He laughed for a long minute. "Me, fly to Montana. That's a good one. Seriously, what am I supposed to do for two weeks by myself?"

Her nose wrinkled in irritation. "I'm sure you'll survive."

"I suppose," he said. "But I'm not going to the theater by myself. Or did you forget we had tickets for next week?"

She blew out a breath. She had forgotten. "I'm sorry. Can't you take one of your friends?"

"I suppose," he said sullenly. "This is so typically Belle, you know? You do whatever works for you and try to fit me in when you have an opening. Good thing for you I'm not ready for something serious yet because, if I were, you would find yourself alone next time you deign to call on me."

"Storm," she started, but he cut her off.

"Forget it. Have fun in Montana," he said derisively and hung up.

"That could have gone better," she murmured. At least the conversation, depressing as it had been, helped pass the lonely miles so by the time she hung up she had reached her exit. The road into town looked exactly the same, as if time had stood still. Maybe it had. If she had stayed here, she would look exactly the same, too. Thank goodness that hadn't happened. If anyone had needed to change, it was Belle Landry.

When she pulled up in front of her parents' house, she was happy to see their home unchanged. Some things needed to remain the same, and her home was one of them. Her Mom ran out to greet her on the porch, arms outstretched for a hug. Belle grinned, bounced from the car, and flew into her mother's arms.

"Oh, I'm so glad you're home," her mother said. "It's about time they let you have a vacation."

Belle's gut twisted with guilt. She received vacation time every year, but she had never taken it. And she wasn't on vacation now; she was working. After stepping out of her mother's embrace, she retrieved her bags from the car and followed her inside.

"Mom, I was thinking about paying a visit to the King ranch today." Belle tried to say it casually, but her mother still gave her a sharp look.

"Are you still pining for Coy?" her mother asked.

Belle's heart twisted at the mention of his name. Funny how something forgotten could be so easily remembered. For as long as she could remember, she'd had a horrible crush on Coy King. And in all that time, he had never looked at her as more than a friend. At least he had been a friend to her, which is more than she could say for some kids.

"I have a boyfriend," she reminded her mother.

"Pfft," her mother blew out a laugh. "Honey, no one can date a man with a name like that. Were his parents hippies?" She gave Belle a narrow-eyed glance. Hippies and Europeans were still feared in these parts for their unconventional sentiments.

"His parents are artists and so is Storm," Belle said.

"Artists," her mother muttered.

"Where's Dad?" Belle asked.

"Where do you think?" her mother replied.

Her family owned the only grocery store in town and her father was almost always working. Even so, the family barely had enough money to get by. The store was small, as was the town, and neither one ever seemed to get ahead in life. Belle had no idea why her parents didn't move somewhere more lucrative. Her father had good business sense. In a larger town, he could have made a killing. But every time Belle tried to talk to them about it, they had the same ready reply: "This is home." Belle didn't understand that notion. To her, home was where she put her hat. Montana had been home for her first seventeen years, and Manhattan had been home for the last four. What was the big deal about moving?

"So, Mom, about visiting the King ranch," Belle began, but her mother interrupted her.

"But you just got here," she said.

I'm also on a deadline, Belle wanted to say. *The sooner I get what I need, the sooner I can get back to civilization.* But looking in her sweet mother's sad eyes, she couldn't bring herself to say the words. Instead, she found herself heading to the kitchen and watching while her mother prepared supper. For tonight, she would visit with her family. And then, first thing in the morning, she would go to the King's ranch and get down to business.

But that didn't happen, either. The next morning, her father wanted to take her to the store and pass her around like his shiny bowling trophy. The cashiers were the same three women who had been working there all of Belle's life, and they did sort of feel like family. They all hugged and exclaimed over her, inundating her with questions about the big city. She spent some time in her dad's office, trying to ignore the fact that his system was woefully outdated, and then she ate lunch with her parents. Her cousin, George, was there and he eyed her suspiciously. With Belle's lack of interest in the family business, George was a shoe-in to replace her father when he retired. Belle had to fight back a laugh over George's insecure reaction.

The store is all yours, George. By the way, I could probably buy it several times over with what I make per year.

Finally at three in the afternoon, she set out on the long journey to the King's ranch. Even though the Kings lived an hour outside of town, they were still considered a part of it. That's the way things were out in the boonies; distance meant nothing. And there were two ways of referring to distance: by road or "as the crow flies"—meaning straight ahead with no curves. Out here, when most people referred to distance that way it meant they were planning to travel by horse or on foot. Belle tried to imagine explaining Montana directions to some of her Manhattan friends and laughed for a long time. The two worlds couldn't be more different.

When she saw the turnoff for the Flying K ranch, her nervousness kicked into overdrive. This was it; she was going to see Coy again after a four-year absence. Would he be as beautiful and perfect as he had once been? Thanks to her mother's overly suspicious nature, Belle had been unable to probe her about the Kings last night. But she knew from previous conversations there were two women living at the ranch now—Cade's girlfriend, and Coy's girlfriend. The arrangement had caused a small scandal in town. Belle knew one of the two women was her author, and she hoped against hope it was Cade's girlfriend. For obvious reasons, she didn't want to work with Coy's girlfriend. In addition to being slightly jealous of the woman, there was also a small part of her that was hoping she might still have a chance with Coy. Maybe when he saw her, he would realize what he had missed out on all these years. Maybe he would send his stupid girlfriend packing in favor of Belle.

It was a ridiculous fantasy, but some dreams died hard. For all of her adolescence, Coy had been Belle's dream. Even though she understood the likelihood he was lost to her forever, there was still a little part of her that mourned for his absence.

At last she reached the end of the long lane. The pretty farmhouse loomed in the distance, exactly as she remembered it. Calling it a farmhouse was probably a stretch. It was more of a mansion, really, with multiple bedrooms, a couple of master suites, and a restaurant-sized kitchen. But the Kings were unpretentious enough to pretend they were on the same level as everybody else in town. As if by some cruel twist of fate, the first person she saw when she stepped out of her rental car was Coy. She would have recognized his beautiful brown curls anywhere, even though they were covered by his Stetson. He rode up to her and dismounted his horse.

"Can I help you, Miss?"

She opened her mouth and no sound came out. He smiled and his beautiful dimple flashed at her. Finally, she squeaked the necessary words through her lips. "It's me, Belle Landry."

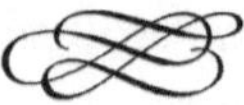

CHAPTER 3

"Belle?" Coy yelled. "Are you kidding me? Is that really you? You look great. It's so good to see you." He beamed at her again before turning to look at the sound of an approaching horse. Belle looked too, and her heart sank. By the look on his face, this was his girlfriend. And, as much as Belle had changed since she left home, she was no competition for this girl. She was beautiful and so perfectly made up she looked like she had just stepped out of a catalogue.

She stopped her horse beside them and looked curiously at Belle. *Please don't let this woman be my author,* Belle thought. She was the most unfriendly, cold-looking person Belle had ever seen. Her blue eyes were icy, and her perfectly arranged light blond hair added to the ice queen effect. Coy reached up and plucked her from the horse, setting her on the ground beside them.

"Ivy, this is our good friend Belle Landry. We haven't seen her since we graduated high school. Belle, this is my wife, Ivy."

"Wife," Belle repeated numbly. Coy was married? How had she missed that piece of gossip?

"We had a whirlwind romance." This came from the ice princess. Only she didn't sound like an ice princess. She had a warm, southern accent, and she was now smiling sweetly at Belle. When Belle held out her hand, Ivy pumped it enthusiastically, grasping it between both her hands and squeezing gently. "I'm so excited to meet you," Ivy said. "I've only met a handful of Coy's friends. Did you travel far? I know you don't live here. I've met everyone in town."

Belle tried to gather her thoughts while chastising herself and feeling like a heel. Coy's wife wasn't an ice princess—she was simply beautiful, so beautiful she was intimidating. But she was obviously a sweetheart. At that moment, any lingering emotions Belle felt for Coy dried up and blew away. It was one thing to have an unrequited crush on another girl's boyfriend, but quite another to feel that way about some woman's husband. No, thank you. Belle wasn't that type of woman.

"Well, well. Look who it is. Hello, Bucky."

Belle had been so absorbed in her thoughts she hadn't noticed Coy's twin brother, Cameron, approach. Now everyone swiveled to look at him.

"Hello, Cam," Belle said coolly, not bothering to reproach him for using her long-outgrown nickname.

"What brings you here?" Cam asked suspiciously.

"I came to shank you in the kidney and take over your ranch," she said. "Can't a girl visit her old friends without a lot of suspicion?"

"Some girls can; you can't. So what's this about, Belle?" He crossed his arms over his chest and regarded her through narrowed eyes.

His distrust galled her, even more so because it was rightfully earned. "I see you're still the same old charmer."

"*You're* not the same. You cut your hair." He reached out to touch the smooth ends of her perfect hair, but she dodged him.

"Don't touch my hair. You know I hate that." His eyes gleamed wickedly and she took a step back. "Don't do it, Cameron." She bumped against the car and there was nowhere to go as he advanced on her and used both hands to ruffle her hair. She smacked his hands away, repeatedly swatting at them like an angry kitten, and he laughed out loud before picking her up with one hand and tucking her under his arm like a football.

"Come into the house and see Cade," he said. Then he carried her up the stairs, leaving Coy and Ivy staring after them.

"Close your mouth," Coy said to Ivy who was staring slack-jawed at the porch.

"What was *that?*" she asked.

"That was Belle Landry," Coy said.

"No, I mean him. I've never seen him act like that with anyone before."

"Yeah, I forgot she has that effect on him," Coy said fondly. He had always had a special place in his heart for Belle.

"Did they ever date?" Ivy asked.

Coy laughed. "No way. It wasn't like that with Belle. She was the one girl we didn't flirt with; the one girl we could be ourselves with. Until Layla came along, she was the closest thing we had to a sister. But she and Cam have always bickered like that. It used to annoy me. Now I think it's sort of funny."

"It's downright amazing," Ivy said. "I've never seen him laugh like that."

"I have. At her. A lot. They know how to push each other's buttons." He smiled toward the house. "I hope she sticks around for a while. This could be fun."

Ivy smiled, too. "Who needs television when you have all the drama a ranch can handle?"

"What drama?" Coy asked. "It's only Belle."

"Wait and see," Ivy said sagely. Then she took his hand and led him into the house.

* * *

CAM PUT Belle down when they reached the house. She shoved away from him with two hands and strode toward the sounds in the kitchen. When she reached it, she wished she had paused to prepare herself for the sight of Cade in his wheelchair. Of course she had heard about his accident and knew he was confined to the chair for life, but hearing about it and seeing it for the first time were two different things.

When they were in high school, she, Coy, and Cam had been in the same class. Cade had been two years behind them, but he and Coy had been close. Because Belle had been friends with Coy and Cam, she had also become friends with Cade. The three of them together had ruled the school, and especially the football field where they had all been on the same team.

Coy had been the quarterback and team captain, but everyone knew Cam called all the shots and told Coy what to do. Cam and Cade had both been receivers and together the brothers had dominated, winning every game that season and taking the school to the state championship.

Now seeing the once-athletic Cade with legs that no longer functioned stole Belle's breath and left her fighting not to cry. Cam came up behind her and draped his arm on her shoulders, providing a handy distraction and a whole lot of annoyance. She tore her eyes off Cade to scowl at Cam as he spoke.

"Look who the cat dragged in," he announced.

Cade and a pretty brown-haired girl turned in the doorway to look at them. They both wore the same expression, as if they were staring at a stranger.

"It's Bucky," Cam announced, tightening his grip on Belle's neck until he had her in a chokehold.

"It's Belle," she said, squirming away from him with another double handed shove. This time she did manage to punch him in the stomach, but it was like punching solid concrete for all the damage she did to him. He didn't even bend over or make a satisfying "oof" sound. In fact he continued to stare at her with smug amusement, inching her annoyance to cosmic levels.

"You've got to be kidding me," Cade blurted, staring at her open-mouthed and unblinking.

Belle ignored the insulting amount of shock in his face and tone by focusing on his girlfriend. She looked like a writer—sort of introverted and dreamy, as if she were often lost in her own world. Belle's heart picked up the pace and she strove to make a good expression on what might be her biggest client to date.

"Hello, I'm Isabelle Landry. I went to high school with these guys, and I stopped in to say hello." Beaming, she held out her hand and took a step forward.

The girl wiped floury hands on a dishtowel before extending her hand to Belle. "I'm Layla," she said, tone friendly and placid. "I'm so pleased to meet you. Won't you stay for supper?"

She started to say she didn't want to intrude, but Cam answered for her.

"Of course she will. Why else would she drop by right at supper time if not to wrangle an invitation?"

Belle put her hands on her hips and turned to face him. "Not everyone eats supper at five in the afternoon, rube. In New York I don't eat supper until eight or nine at night. Have some sophistication, why don't you?"

"But you're not in New York, elitist control freak, you're in Montana, and unless you've taken a significant blow to the head and wound up with amnesia, you know everyone eats early here." He pointed to the ground beneath him, as if he somehow needed to clarify where they were.

She had forgotten how early everyone ate, but it was pointless to argue with Cameron King, which was one more thing that hadn't changed about home. The thought was oddly comforting. She turned her back on him and faced Layla again, putting up her hand like a shield to block Cam and his obnoxiously smug smile. "I really wasn't thinking about supper when I set out here, and I would feel horrible to impose. I'm sure my mother has supper prepared."

"But it's an hour back to town," Cade said. "We would love to have you join us. Layla always cooks too much, even for us. Please? I want to hear what you've been up to."

"Please," Layla added, clasping her hands under her chin in an adorable manner Belle had never been able to pull off. If she ever tried she would likely look like she was about to use her hands to double club someone with them. "Do you need to call your mother?"

"I have my cell phone," she said, pulling it from her pocket.

Cam laughed. "Wow, you have been gone a long time. No please, go ahead," he said when she paused mid-dial to glare at him.

When she heard the familiar message telling her there was no signal, she understood his amusement. Of course there was no cell service out here in the remotest part of her remote hometown. How had she forgotten? "I'll call her later," she said casually, pretending her connection had been fine as she pushed her phone back in her pocket.

Cam laughed again, shaking his head. "Same old Bucky."

No, she wasn't. So despite the fact that her hands clenched into fists at her sides, demanding retribution, she ignored his taunts. As if a magic and silent dinner bell had sounded, Josh, Coy and Ivy appeared in the kitchen and sat at the table. Josh was another surprise for Belle. At four years younger, she had always thought of him as a baby. But now he stood shoulder to shoulder with his brothers. His hair was almost as light in color as Cam's, but he had two deep dimples. Cam had one, but he smiled so rarely few people knew about it.

"Why do you call her Bucky?" Josh asked.

"Because when I was in elementary school, my permanent teeth came in too big for my face," Belle answered placidly.

"But your teeth are beautiful," Ivy said.

"Thanks to the miracle of orthodontia."

"There's an orthodontist here?" Layla asked.

"No," everyone answered at once.

"I had to go to the city once a week," Belle answered. "I had to go to the city for *everything*," she added.

"Like what?" Josh said.

"Piano lessons, writing class, dance class," Belle listed, counting on her fingers the town's deficiencies.

"You took dance class?" Cam interrupted.

"Why do you sound so surprised?"

"Because I've never seen you dance," he said.

Most likely that was due to the fact that she had never attended a school dance during all of high school. "If I had known you were interested in attending one of my recitals, I would have invited you," she said.

"And wouldn't you have been surprised if I attended?" he retorted.

Yes, she would have been. They had been friends at school because they had several classes together, but they hadn't hung out. Previously she had only been to this house at Coy's invitation. Coy had been a true friend to her; Cam had merely tolerated her presence. She smiled wryly, thinking once again how some things never changed.

CHAPTER 4

*O*ver supper, Belle asked questions about other people they went to school with. Not that she cared about any of them because she didn't. But it seemed polite to inquire. Not surprisingly, none of them had left town.

"What's Marissa up to?" Belle asked.

"She married Pete. They have two kids."

The young marrying and birthing ages were something else that bothered Belle about her hometown.

"Why do you look like you swallowed broken glass?" Cam asked. "Don't tell me you had a crush on Pete, too."

She ignored the "too." He had always known about her feelings for Coy. "No, I didn't have a crush on Pete. I've simply grown used to people who don't think about marriage until their thirties. What's the rush? We're so young." She shook her head, pitying the poor yokels, not remembering until later Coy and Ivy were similarly young and married.

"And then by the time they're ready for kids, they're so old they have to go to a doctor for help getting pregnant," Cam added, the disdain in his tone matching hers but for vastly different reasons. Of course he would hate all things urban. Everyone did here, apparently.

Begrudgingly, Belle thought of Nancy who had been almost forty when she decided she wanted to have a baby. She had spent close to a hundred thousand dollars on fertility treatments before using a surrogate. "Lots of young people have problems with fertility, too," she said, unwilling to admit there was any truth in his cynical statement. "Were you heartbroken over Marissa? I seem to remember you eating your heart out over her when she turned you down for prom." She took a bite of her beans, shooting him an acid smile.

"You didn't tell me you asked Marissa to prom," Coy said, tossing his twin an annoyed glance. Belatedly Belle remembered that Coy had taken Marissa to prom. "I wouldn't have asked her if I knew you liked her."

"Wouldn't you?" Cam asked. Again he sounded cynical. An awkward pall settled over the room. Belle had no idea why, and she sensed something other than prom was the cause. She cleared her throat. All attention swiveled expectantly to her.

"At least we finished the yearbook that night," she said. She and Cam shared a smile. It was a rare, genuine smile on his part, causing his peekaboo dimple to flash and Belle's heart melted with a bit of nostalgia for old times. Since neither she nor Cam had a date for prom their senior year, they had decided to stage a coup and take over the yearbook committee. They spent the evening rearranging everything that had been done that year by the other members of the committee. No one was happy when they found out about it, but everyone was too afraid of the combination of Belle and Cam to do anything about it. If she were being honest, prom night with him— spent laboriously poring over the yearbook—ended up being one of the best nights of her high school career, fun enough that she hadn't felt sad at what else she was missing.

With more difficulty than she would have imagined possible, she ripped her attention from a still-smiling Cam to the other two women at the table. One of them was a potential client, and now was the time to start laying the groundwork.

"So all of you live here together like one big, happy family," she said lightly.

"For now," Coy said. "Ivy and I are renovating the old homestead."

"And Layla and I are building a house that's fully handicapable," Cade said.

"Are you engaged?" Belle asked.

There was another awkward silence.

"Uh-oh. That was nosy. I'm sorry," she apologized.

"No, it's okay," Layla said. "We're not engaged. We're…committed," she finished lamely.

Definitely don't go there again, Belle told herself. Maybe Cade had commitment issues. Whatever the cause, it was a touchy subject. Before she could ask further questions, Ivy turned the tables on her.

"What do you do, Belle? Coy said you live in New York."

"Yes, I live in Manhattan." She took a bite of food and chewed, trying to stall. Instinctively she knew if she blurted out her career whichever one of them was the writer might become suspicious. "I'm an agent."

"Like a sports agent?" Josh asked excitedly, the first thing he'd said in a while.

"She's a literary agent," Cam volunteered deadpan. "Your parents fill me in on your life every time I'm in town," he added to her.

"I can only imagine," Belle said. Surreptitiously, she glanced at Ivy and Layla, noting their reactions to the news of her job. Both of them were watching her with large, curious eyes, and neither looked like they wanted to run screaming from the room. Maybe she had misconstrued their reticence. Maybe this was going to be easier than she thought. "What do you guys do?" she asked them.

"Ivy is our breeder extraordinaire," Coy said proudly.

Now it was Ivy's turn to wrinkle her nose and blush delicately, a fact that did nothing to diminish her over-the-top perfection. If Belle were the type of person to blush, she would no doubt turn immediately puce, like someone who was choking on a grape. "*Horse* breeder. He always forgets to add that part; it makes me sound like I'm in a back room somewhere birthing multiple children for money."

Belle chortled at the unexpected response. Ivy was definitely likeable. Right away Belle could tell she would be pleasant to work with. Her eyes swung to Layla. "And what about you?"

For some reason, the question brought tears to Layla's eyes. "I'm the housekeeper," she said. Cade reached for her, but she stood. "Excuse me." She pushed back her chair and exited the room. With a frustrated sigh, Cade wheeled himself from the room after her.

"I'm stepping in it all over the place here," Belle muttered.

"It's not your fault; it's ours," Ivy said sadly. "They've been dating for a long time, and yet somehow we were married first. I'm afraid it's made things a little touchy between them."

"And since Ivy moved in and started taking up her breeding operation, I think Layla feels a little insignificant in her position as housekeeper. Not that any of us feel that way," Coy hastened to add. "She doesn't seem to understand she's family and we love her no matter what. I think she feels like she wants to do something more with her life."

"She could go to college," Belle suggested.

"We don't want her to leave," Josh piped up. He sounded young and more than a little desperate at the thought of Layla going away.

"She wouldn't have to leave. She could get her degree online. Or she could take a class once a week in the city. There are lots of options."

"That's true," Cam agreed thoughtfully. "Maybe I can talk to her about them."

"Or maybe I can," Belle said, seeing an opportunity and deciding to take it. If Layla was the writer, maybe she had already found the outlet she needed and was too insecure about it to let the rest of her family know what she was up to.

"I don't know about that," Cam said, disapproval ringing in his tone.

Belle frowned. "What are you afraid of, Cameron—that I'll make her into my mini me?"

"Yes," he said. "I don't want Layla getting any ideas about becoming too big for her britches and going away."

"Too big for her... Never mind, that's too much yokel to dispute.

Maybe she wants to go away. It's a big world out there," Belle said. She had only been here a day, and she was already tired of the inbred, small-minded attitudes.

"She's already seen the big world," Cam snapped, apparently as annoyed with her as she was with him. "She's from Chicago. She came to us in the witness protection program, and she doesn't have anyone besides us."

"Oh," Belle drawled, blinking rapidly at him, even though he wasn't the object of her focus. Layla was looking more and more like the best possibility here. She had apparently had a colorful life before she came here. That alone would give her plenty to draw from as a writer. Belle's mind was already jumping ahead to contracts and legalities.

"Should I do the dishes?" Ivy asked, staring at the sink. "I never know what's best so I don't upset her more."

"I'll do the dishes," Belle volunteered. She pushed aside her plate and stood. The food was good, but much heavier than she was used to. After only a few bites she was full. Plus it would give her an excuse to linger. That way if Layla came back she would have a good opportunity to talk to her.

"I'll help," Cam surprised everyone by volunteering.

Josh and Coy vacated the room before they could get sucked into dish duty, taking Ivy with them until only Cam and Belle remained in the room. For a few minutes they worked in oddly comfortable silence, ferrying dishes to the sink.

"Sounds like there's tension at the old homestead," Belle said at last. "I'm sorry if I stirred everything up by coming here."

"You didn't," Cam said easily. "Things have been tense all around since Coy and Ivy's wedding."

"What's Cade waiting for? He obviously loves Layla. Does he have commitment issues?"

"In a manner of speaking," Cam said. "He doesn't think they're old enough to get married, and he feels like he needs to have a certain amount in the bank before he takes on a wife. But of course Layla doesn't see it that way. She thinks he's stalling because he's having second thoughts about her."

"But that's crazy. She's beautiful and sweet, and he's obviously in love with her."

"Who can understand what goes on in the mind of a woman?" Cam said, grinning at her.

"You're trying to bait me. It won't work. I've grown up," she said proudly.

Cam laughed. "You're still the same Belle Landry as ever, and I see right through you. You're here because you want something."

"What could I possibly want here?" she asked innocently.

"Coy?" he ventured. One eyebrow cocked as he studied her.

She scowled at him. "If you think that, then you never knew me."

"I know you had a crush on him almost from birth."

"That was then. This is now."

"What's changed? And don't tell me it's you because I know better," he said.

"He's *married*. Give me a little credit."

"And if he wasn't married?" Cam asked.

She ground her teeth at his mocking tone. "That's a moot point and I won't go there. Besides, I have a boyfriend."

"Did you tie him up to keep him at your parents' house today?" he asked.

"No, he's in New York," she replied with exaggerated patience.

"So you're not serious," he guessed.

"We're as serious as I want to be," she said.

"What does that mean?"

They had been clearing the table and stacking the dishes while they talked. Now she began to wash and he held out his hand to take a plate from her. The strange thing about her relationship with Cam was that—after all the annoyance with each other cleared away— they'd always been able to talk to each other. They got each other somehow, and even when she wanted to kill him she felt like he understood her. It was odd, she thought, how easily she resumed that old comfort with him, like putting on a favorite pair of slippers.

"It means I'm laser focused on my career. Any relationship I'm in right now has to take a back seat to that."

"And he's okay with that?" he asked.

"What man wouldn't be? I'm there when he wants me and gone when he doesn't," she said.

He shook his head. She felt disapproval rolling off him in waves.

"Dare I ask why you're shaking your head like that?" she said.

"I'm shaking my head at you, Belle. You're still trying to arrange the world to your satisfaction."

"As I remember, you were pretty good at that yourself," she said.

"You're right. And look how well that turned out. Soon I'll be living in this house alone, spending my days with computers and cows. Meanwhile, my brother married my girlfriend and is living happily ever after."

She froze and stared at him, open-mouthed. "Ivy was your girlfriend?"

He stared out the window as he answered and she wondered if he hadn't meant to impart that information. Maybe he was similarly surprised at how easy it was to talk to her, too. "We weren't serious. We met online and talked for about a year. I brought her out here to see how things went in person. But then she and Coy were stranded in a snowstorm for a few days. One thing led to another and—bing—four weeks later they were married."

She set down the dish and surprised them both by laying her hand comfortingly on his forearm. "I'm sorry, Cam. That really stinks."

He shrugged, his fingers smoothing absently over hers, staring at them as he spoke. "She and I weren't in love. They were. End of story."

But it wasn't the end of the story; she knew better. At the very least, his pride had been lanced. Knowing this town the way she did, she knew everyone would have known the story. Now everyone viewed Cam as the jilted brother, the one who hadn't been good enough for Ivy. And even if he hadn't been in love with her, she had once been his. Now she wasn't and he had to see her under his roof every day, rubbing salt in his wound. At least the odd tension in the atmosphere was beginning to make sense. Coy and Ivy's impromptu marriage had thrown a monkey wrench in the family dynamic in more ways than one.

They finished the dishes in silence and she turned to face him. What she was about to do would surprise both of them, but suddenly it seemed imperative. Cam needed a dose of spontaneous fun in her life as much as she did, maybe more. "You want to get out of here?" she asked.

"Where to?" he asked, quirking an eyebrow, one lip tilted in preemptive amusement.

"Oh, I think you know," she said. His answering smile told her he did. He threw the dishtowel on the counter, tossed Belle over his shoulder, and ran out the door, laughing like a kid all the way to the car.

CHAPTER 5

They took Cam's old farm truck because it wouldn't matter if they came back filthy, which they undoubtedly would.

"I can't even remember the last time I was at this place. It was probably when I was with you that day," Cam said.

"That's definitely the last time I was there," Belle said. "Are we crazy for doing this?"

"Yes, but right now being crazy feels good," he said. "Thanks for reminding me about this place."

"I can't believe you forgot. It's on your land."

"Yes, but there hasn't been much reason to go since you went away."

"Since I beat you, you mean," she said.

He gave an exaggerated sigh. "You always did have a creative memory, Bucky."

If she told him to stop calling her that, he would no doubt keep it up to annoy her further. But the temptation was so great to lash out at him that she literally had to bite her tongue. He stopped the truck and shifted it into park.

"Ready?" he asked.

"As I'll ever be," she said warily. It was September. Although it had been warm when she left New York, September in Montana was always freezing and today was no exception. By Montana standards, though, it was actually almost balmy at fifty degrees.

"Come on, don't chicken out on me now," he said, knowing those would be the magic words to propel her out of the truck. He reached across the seat and pinched her waist.

"I'm not a chicken," she said, slamming out of the truck. He smiled as he exited the truck and trotted behind her. They stopped at the bank and stared at the water below, but it was too dark to see anything.

"Are you sure it's still deep enough?" she asked.

"I'm sure," he said.

"How can you be sure when you haven't been here in four years?"

"I know my land," he said confidently. "The creek would have changed if the spring had drained. If anything, it's deeper than it was. Want me to go first and prove it's safe?" He was taunting her again, but he couldn't help it. No one's buttons had ever been as fun to push as Belle Landry's, and tonight was no exception. The unexpected appearance of the smartest, most stubbornly driven person he'd ever known felt like some kind of gift in the midst of what had been a difficult season for him. She frowned at him as she gingerly took off her sweater. She stood before him in a bra that was as modest as any bikini, probably more so, but he still found it hard not to gawk. Belle Landry. Two feet away. In her bra. Heavens.

"This is cashmere," she said grudgingly.

"This is flannel," he said as he began unbuttoning his shirt.

"And you have twenty more exactly like it in your closet," she said.

"Eighteen, actually. I donated a couple to charity."

They removed their excess clothing and stood looking over the bank again in their skivvies, both trying not to let the other see them shiver, both trying hard not to peek. "What was my record four years ago?" she asked, teeth chattering a heartening amount.

"One minute, forty five seconds."

She smiled. "Correct me if I'm wrong, but that beat your time by three seconds, correct?"

"You know it did," he said tightly. "But that was then. This is now. And it was also summer, and you had been swimming a lot that year. Been swimming lately, Bucky?"

"No. Have you?"

"Touché," he said. "Ready?"

"You already asked me that," she snapped.

"And yet you're still standing here." *In your bra and underwear. Have mercy, she looks better than I remember.* "Bock, bock." He tucked his hands under his armpits and flapped his arms.

She narrowed her eyes at him a second before jumping off the bank and doing a cannonball into the unseen depths below. The water was shockingly, numbingly cold. They would only be able to stay in long enough for the competition before hypothermia set in. Maybe it would set in even before then. All she knew was she was the coldest she had ever been, and every instinct screamed at her to get out of the water as soon as possible.

"Look out below, I'm coming down," Cam yelled.

She forced her frozen muscles to dog paddle a few feet away from the center of the small pond and made it out of the way a split second before Cam landed with a loud splash right behind her.

"Y-y-you m-made m-me j-jump f-first on p-purpose so I w-w-would be fr-freezing by the t-time you g-got here," she accused.

"Ah, you know me too well, Bucky. You ready? Ladies first." He held his watch out of the water and pushed a button to illuminate the dial. "On my count: ready, set, go."

She took a deep breath and ducked under the water. Immediately, her lungs screamed for release. She held them off by concentrating on how good it would feel to beat Cam at something. She knew because she had beaten him at this very competition four years ago. He had been so smug when he issued the challenge, so sure un-athletic Belle Landry would never be able to beat his football playing self at anything. But she had. And she would do it again, or die trying. She waited until she felt like she was going to die and then stayed down a second after that. As she surfaced, she gasped for breath, sure she would never be warm again.

"Wh-what was m-my t-time?" she asked.

"One minute forty six seconds. Impressive."

"Y-yoga," she said.

"I could have guessed it was something like that. When you start my time, push here. Got it?"

"P-push th-that button. Could you wr-write that down f-for me?"

"Hilarious." He took a breath and ducked under the water, holding his arm up. She grasped his wrist and pushed the button, staring at the button and willing it not to move so her new record time would remain undefeated. And then with mounting anger she watched as his time approached and surpassed hers. And still he didn't surface. After two minutes, her anger turned to concern, and then to panic.

"Cam," she called, looking down into the inky water below. She couldn't see or hear a thing. She was still holding his arm, but it felt icy and limp. She began tugging on it, but to no avail. "Please, please, please," she muttered. For some reason, she was compelled to glance at his watch. He had been under for almost three minutes. Swallowing down rising panic, she tugged harder on his arm, but there was no way she could lift dead weight out of the water from above. So, taking another huge breath, she dove below the surface, put her arms around his inert form, and lifted with all her might.

Her face was very close to his as they came to the surface of the water. And that was when she saw it. A large reed was stuck between his lips and bent at an angle.

"I win," he said.

"You cheated. You were breathing the whole time. For shame, and you, a landowner."

"Technically, we never specified the rules, Bucky."

"If my limbs were able to function, I could seriously kill you right now. I thought you were dead, you big jerk."

He probably couldn't hear her tirade over the sound of his laughter, but she felt better for yelling at him. She began to swim away from him toward where she thought the bank was, but he put his arm around her waist and pulled her back.

"You're going the wrong way," he said. His breath was warm on her chilly neck, causing her to shiver convulsively.

"Which way is it?" she asked tightly. She hated that she had to ask, but she was disoriented.

"Here." He swam on his back toward the embankment behind him. Instead of letting her go, he pulled her along with him and helped her out of the water when they reached the edge. She would never in a million years admit she needed the help because her muscles were too frozen to haul herself out.

"Cheater," she said instead, collapsing on the bank beside him. "Shameless scoundrel. Rogue. Villain. Miscreant. My record stands intact."

"So you say," he said.

Shakily, she drew herself on her elbows to look down at him. She pressed a palm to his smooth, wet—and impressively sculpted—chest. "Cam, the one thing you've always had going for you is your honesty. Don't lose that. Admit I won, or else."

He smiled up at her despite the fact that her wet hair was pelting his face with heavy droplets of freezing spring water. "Or else what?"

"I'll think of something," she said cryptically.

He had no doubt she would. Isabelle Landry had always been a formidable opponent. He had no doubt she was very good at whatever she did now. She had always been the type of girl who didn't let anything or anyone stand in her way. Focused, determined, smart and sassy, she had never fit in with the other girls. If not for Coy taking pity on her, she would have been a loner. But his brother had always had a soft spot for the buck-toothed, frizzy-haired, bespectacled little oddball.

Cam had never understood what Coy saw in her, but he was beginning to. Not that she looked the same as she had when they were in high school. No, she had gone to New York and had a total makeover, that was for certain. Now her once frizzy hair was tame and smooth, falling below her chin. Gone was the mousy brown color, and in its place was a rich chestnut hue with gold highlights. He supposed her eyes had always been the same pretty shade of brown rimmed in gold, but he had never seen them because they were always stuck behind her Coke bottle frames. Her teeth had been straightened before she left home, so that was no surprise. But now she was decked head to toe in matching designer clothes. She looked pretty and polished. But despite the fact that she looked nothing like the girl she had been, he had no trouble recognizing her when he stepped out of his office earlier in the day. There was something in her body language that had always been easily identifiable to him, as if she were facing a crowd of enemies and would take them all on bare fisted and with every intention of winning.

Seeing her again had triggered something in him, something he had long suppressed: the desire to have fun. Once he had been a regular kid like everyone else. Long before he became the boss of his family's ranch, he had been a boy who competed with this girl for every blasted thing in his life. She had beaten him for valedictorian by one tenth of a percentage point on a calculus test. He had always found it surprising she didn't don a football uniform and challenge him on the field, too, but that was probably because most of his memories of her included a lot of falling on her part. He wondered if she still had two left feet and smiled up at her, remembering a few of her more humiliating collisions.

While he had been recollecting the past and the new changes in Belle, she had let go his chest and lay in the grass on her back, shivering uncontrollably, teeth chattering so loudly they sounded like castanets.

"Let's go to the truck where it's warm," he suggested.

"Can't. Too cold to move," she mumbled between clacking teeth.

He surprised them both by rolling toward her and draping his arm over her, drawing her slight torso against his solid one, bestowing warmth. He hadn't ever been a demonstrative person, and especially not with a girl he hadn't seen since high school, one who was now clad only in her underwear. Her *wet* underwear. "Come on. We'll go back to the house and have hot cocoa."

She laughed and turned her face toward him, amused by offer that was so unlike him. "With baby marshmallows?"

"If you want," he said, returning her smile with something that felt a whole like affection. Belle Landry was turning out to be an unexpected surprise in the midst of an otherwise dreary day.

They lay looking at each other for a few minutes in silence, each one noting the subtle changes that had taken place in the space of four years. At least in his case the changes were subtle. For all intents and purposes, he might have graduated the day before. Belle was the one who had changed monumentally. But for all that she was pretty now, he found he rather missed the skinny little nerd she had been. At least then he had known where he stood with her. With this sophisticated stranger, he was a little out of his element.

"Tell me I won and I'll go back to the house," she said.

He tipped his head to the side, studying her. *There's the Belle I know.* "I'll say it on one condition."

"What's that?" she asked, wary now.

"Promise to come back tomorrow."

CHAPTER 6

Belle lay staring at him, unblinking. "Why?" It wasn't her fault she sounded suspicious. An invitation to return was possibly the last thing she expected.

He shrugged. "I don't know. It's been fun, like old times."

"But we weren't exactly besties then," she pointed out.

"No, but we still had fun sometimes."

That was true. They were possibly the only two people on the planet who understood each other and sometimes that had created a sort of camaraderie between them. Their relationship was similar to two spies who found themselves in a time of peace with each other. They remained wary and cautious, but each had an understanding and sympathy for what the other was going through. While Belle was puzzling through his invitation, looking for hidden agendas, she realized he had offered her exactly what she needed—the chance to return and find what she was looking for. She also realized his palm was still pressed to her stomach and that was probably the reason she was no longer shaking with cold.

"You're hot," she blurted.

He blinked at her a few times. "This is an unexpected turn of events."

"Not like that," she said impatiently. "I mean your hand on my stomach is warm. Feels nice. But I'm not sure it's healthy for anyone to be so freakishly hot. You're like a furnace."

He gave her the wicked grin she was coming to expect from him before he did something to either embarrass or annoy her. "That's why I sleep naked."

It was worse than she expected. She slapped both palms over her eyes.

"What are you doing?" he asked, clearly amused.

"Trying not to picture it. You can't say things like that to me."

"You're a sophisticated New Yorker now. You can't tell me that talking about showing a little skin embarrasses you."

"I can and I am."

"But you're lying here in your bra and underpants."

"Don't say underpants. And I had no choice. Do you know how much my cashmere sweater and wool pants cost? More than any of your ranch doohickies, that's for certain."

"It's really okay, Belle. I'm a rancher. I'm comfortable talking about the circle of life and se…" He would have continued but she slapped her hand over his mouth.

"Please, I'm begging you to drop this line of conversation and never mention it again. And go to church on Sunday or I'm calling your mother." With that, she sprang up and sprinted to the truck, leaving him lying on the ground laughing until his stomach hurt.

He retrieved their dry clothes from the bank and leisurely strolled to the truck. Inwardly, he was delighting in the fact that Belle was as innocent as the day she'd left Montana. He hadn't been certain what he was dealing with when she stripped to her skivvies so casually, but apparently preserving her fancy clothes was worth any price. Belle was still Montana levels of modest and shy. He wasn't sure why that should make him happy, but it did.

"I picked up your sweater," he announced as he opened the door.

"Thank you," she said primly, setting it on the seat beside her.

"Aren't you going to put it on?" he asked. "I thought you were freezing."

"I am, but I told you it's cashmere. I don't want to get it dirty with your stinky spring water."

He cast his eyes toward the top of the truck. "Girls and their clothes," he mumbled before tossing his flannel shirt at her. "Then put this on. The sound of your teeth chattering is annoying, and we can't exactly show up at the ranch with you in a wet bra."

"And you don't have a girlfriend why?" she asked sarcastically.

"Who says I don't?" he returned.

That was true; he had never said if he was dating someone. "I guess I assumed that after your brother married your girlfriend you would want to take a break."

"You assumed correctly," he told her. "After Ivy, it's back to the drawing board."

"What does that mean?"

"It means I know what I'm looking for, and I won't be happy until I find it."

"What are you looking for? And keep in mind that if the phrase 36-24-36 comes up at any time in this conversation, you'll have to pull over while I throw up."

He laughed. "No, nothing like that."

She crossed her arms and gave him a squinty-eyed look.

"Okay, that would definitely be a bonus, but that's not what I'm talking about."

"Then what are you talking about?"

"Well, she has to like Montana. She has to be okay with the lack of modernity and isolation. She has to come from a reliable family. I would like her to be able to add something to the business. A sense of humor is a plus, and she has to be okay with the fact that I go on the range for days at a time or stay in my office working until all hours. I would like for her to be pretty. And a good cook. And a good potential mother for my children. It would be important to know whether insanity runs in her family." He stared through the windshield, trying to remember if there was something he was missing from his list.

"And of course you would want to have your vet make sure her teeth are sound," Belle added sarcastically. "Although nowadays I hear a lot of breeders do genetic testing on their herds. That should answer a lot of your questions. Oh, I'm sorry, were you not talking about a horse? I got confused during your spiel."

"Dating advice from the woman who doesn't care whether or not her boyfriend is a few thousand miles away." Now it was his turn to sound sarcastic.

She sighed. "You're right. We're both messed up in that department. But at least I'm willing to admit it. You still think you're on track with your creepy, creepy list."

He jerked the wheel to the right, causing her to bonk her head on the window. She leaped across the seat and jerked the wheel in the other direction, causing him to bump his head on his window.

"That hurt," she said angrily. Neither of them had any fear of hitting anything because they were in the middle of a large field. *Score one for Montana traffic,* she thought.

Without losing momentum, he took his right foot off the gas pedal and moved his left over to cover it. He secured his right arm around Belle's waist and pressed his right leg over both her legs to keep her from kicking.

"Dang it, Belle. That hurt. You're such a…"

"A what?" she asked, prepared to brawl over his answer.

His eyes scraped her up and down, lingering a little too long. "You're such a woman."

Her lashes fluttered and she faced forward. "Serves you right, you irritating cowboy."

He laughed, but didn't loosen his grip until they arrived back at the house.

* * *

COY AND IVY were on the porch, holding hands and talking while they sat on the swing. No one had any idea where Belle and Cam had disappeared to, but nothing prepared them for the sight of the soaking wet couple pulling up to the house in the old farm truck. They were practically sharing a seat and Cam had his arm tucked firmly around Belle. To top it off, Belle was wearing Cam's flannel shirt.

"Oh, wow," Coy whispered. "It's times like these I'm glad we don't have neighbors."

"See, I told you," Ivy whispered smugly. "There's no drama like ranch drama."

Cam exited the truck, hauled Belle out, and threw her over his shoulder like a sack of potatoes. "You guys want some hot cocoa?" he called. "I owe Bucky a cup after I beat her at holding my breath. With baby marshmallows." Those were the last coherent words he uttered before Belle's foot connected solidly with his sternum.

He set her down and stumbled back against the truck, clutching his heart. Belle swept past him, her arms crossed irritably over her chest.

"He's fine," she told Coy and Ivy as they stared at him in concern. "Trust me when I tell you he's unkillable."

A soft chuckle from Cam convinced them her words were true. He sprinted up the steps behind her. With another puzzled glance at each other, Ivy and Coy turned and followed them into the house.

Cade and Layla had apparently made up because they were in the kitchen, talking and laughing together over cups of coffee. They, too, froze at the sight of a wet Belle, Cam's shirt draping almost to her knees.

"Are you okay?" Layla asked, noting Belle's blue lips and angry expression.

"She's fine," Cam said breathlessly behind her. "She usually looks that angry."

"But not that blue," Coy added. "What have you guys been up to, or do I want to know?"

"We went swimming," Cam said.

Everyone turned to look at him, trying to figure out if he was serious.

"I went swimming," Belle said. "He went cheating." She turned to glare at him. "Cheater. Cad. Rounder. Shame on you."

He rolled his eyes and sank to the table. "Fine. You won. Are you happy?"

She smiled triumphantly and sank down beside him. "Yes, actually." And then she chafed her hands up and down her arms, shuddering convulsively. Cam rose, retrieved an afghan from the living room, and wrapped it around her shoulders, giving it a tug before sitting down once again.

"Thanks," Belle said quietly, conscious of the fact that the rest of the family was still staring at them. And also suddenly conscious of the fact that the two other females in the room were perfectly groomed while she was wet, blue, frizzy, and wearing ill-fitting flannel.

"I should go," she said, starting to rise.

Cam caught her wrist and tugged her gently back down. "I promised you cocoa." He started to rise, but Layla beat him to it.

"I'll make it," she said. "Does everyone else want some?" Everyone said they did. She bit her lip and looked down the hall. "Do you think we should wake Josh and ask him if he wants some?"

"Nah," Cade said. "Let him sleep. He has a test tomorrow."

"Does he graduate this year?" Belle asked.

"He does," Coy said.

"Unbelievable," she replied. "I still think of him as such a baby. It's kind of amazing he didn't go wild, living here two years without parental supervision."

"It's obvious you don't know Josh at all," Cade said. "Wild is not in his vocabulary."

"He's a good kid," Cam said with obvious pride.

"It must have been hard on your parents to be away from you guys these last couple of years," Belle commented. Once again, a heavy silence settled over the room. "Oh, geez, not again," she muttered, making everyone laugh.

"It's been hard on all of us," Coy volunteered. "But Dad's arthritis has been doing better without these Montana winters to contend with, and that's what counts."

She nodded, trying to picture their hale and hearty father diminished in any way. She had seen the effects of rheumatoid arthritis, but still couldn't picture the elder Mr. King as anything but the robust and jolly man she remembered.

They sat and talked over cocoa for the next hour and a half, until Belle's blinks became longer and farther between.

"I should go. Thanks for tonight, guys. It was great to see you and get caught up." She dashed a significant look toward Layla and Ivy. "And it was lovely to meet the new additions. I hope to get to know you better in the little time I have left."

"Are you dying?" Cam asked.

"You wish," she said. She tossed the afghan in his face and pushed back her chair.

He laughed and stood, too. "I'll walk you out."

They left the kitchen, oblivious to the fact that the rest of the family was staring at them in silent wonder.

"Come earlier tomorrow," Cam commanded as soon as they were on the porch.

"Yes, your majesty," she agreed, feigning meekness.

"I prefer Your Royal Highness, if we're being formal," he said.

She stopped at her car and faced him. "I hate to admit it, but I actually had fun with you tonight."

"Me too. The hating to admit it part, I mean."

She rolled her eyes and shivered.

"How can you still be cold?" he asked, frowning in concern. Maybe she had lost her Montana hardiness. Maybe she would actually get sick now. Who knew what the city had done to her?

"I just am. It's part of being human, I guess. You should try it someti…"

Before he could think about it too much, he wrapped his arms around her, cutting off her flow of words. Her arms crossed over her chest, trapped like a mummy, and she blinked up at him in surprise.

"Are you going to be okay to drive home?" he murmured. "You could stay here if you want."

"That's actually very sweet of you, but I have no desire to get tangled up in your family's shameful web of intrigue."

He grimaced. "People in town are talking, huh?"

"Oh, yeah. I've gotten quite the earful. These are the days of the King's lives."

"*Ugh*. But you've seen for yourself we're pretty innocent out here. Nothing sinister is going on. You can spread the word."

"Fat lot of good it would do. People love intrigue," she said. Especially here where there was nothing else going on. "You're very hot," she added.

"Thank you kindly. A man can't hear that enough."

"You know what I mean. I'm actually warm now. It's like magic."

"Then give me back my shirt." He removed his arms from around her and began unbuttoning the shirt she was wearing.

She batted his hands away. "Stop trying to take my clothes off. I'll bring your shirt back tomorrow, Strippy McGee." With that she opened her door, slid into the car, and drove away. Cam stood in the driveway a long time after she was gone, smiling at nothing.

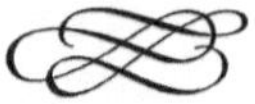

CHAPTER 7

*B*elle woke the next morning with a renewed sense of purpose. Last night she had allowed misplaced sentimentality over her reunion with Cam to divert her from her task, but not today. Today she was going to find her author and sign her. Maybe after that she would spend a few minutes with Cam doing whatever it was he wanted her to do.

Three of her electronic devices beeped, alerting her to the fact that she had messages out the wazoo. But if she started checking them now it would take all day. No, today she had bigger fish to fry. Studiously ignoring the messages, she jumped out of bed, dressed, and spent some time with her mother.

Besides the fact that she had missed her mother, it was good to try and throw her off the scent of her real purpose for being here. For that reason, it was noon when she set out toward the King ranch. Noon to ranchers was almost like the end of the day because they rose so early, so she felt fairly confident Cam would be far and away by the time she arrived. She was wrong.

He walked down the porch steps and met her at her car as soon as she exited. "Good, you're here. I was getting ready to go. Come on." He scooped her up by the waist and pulled her backward, her arms and legs still extended toward the house, reaching.

"But I want to go inside and say hello to the ladies," she protested.

"The ladies aren't here," he said, offering no further explanation of where they might have gone. He carried her to what looked like a golf cart on steroids and stuffed her unceremoniously inside.

"You know, I'm able to walk places on my own two feet," she said.

"Where's the fun in that?" He started the car and set out.

"Where are you taking me?" she asked.

"We're checking on a cow."

"Why aren't we taking horses?"

"I was under the impression you didn't care for horses," he said.

He was correct. She didn't have much experience with the animals except the times she had tried to ride here. She had fallen off. Twice. If the amused smirk on his face was any indication, he was also remembering the times she fell off. He glanced at her and caught her staring at him before reaching over to squeeze her knee. She jumped and pushed his hand off.

"Don't tickle me," she said.

He quirked an eyebrow at her. "You're ticklish?"

"No," she lied. "I'm dead inside."

"Join the club," he said. They drove for a while in silence until they reached wherever it was they were, then he turned off the engine and stared at the large cow in front of them.

"What are we looking for?" she asked.

"Signs of distress," he said.

"Like a suicide note or manifesto?" she guessed.

He spared her a glance before turning back to the cow.

Because the cow looked like every other cow she had ever seen, she closed her eyes and rested her legs on the top of the vehicle, stretching them out in front of her to soak up the sun.

Cam shattered the peaceful silence by speaking. "Tell me about your boyfriend. What's he like?"

"He's an artist," she began, but didn't get far because he snickered.

"Is that code for unemployed?"

"No, he's actually successful enough to support himself. Not many artists can say that."

"Is he one of those who splashes a little paint on a canvas and sells it for a million dollars?"

"No. He does landscapes. City landscapes," she clarified. "They're actually quite lovely. Architecture in New York is captivating. He specializes in night scenes." His work was what first drew her to him. She had been at an art gallery staring at one of his more morose pieces, feeling lonely because of the single light in the painting when he happened beside her and introduced himself.

"Is he our age?"

"No, he's older."

"How old?"

"Thirty."

He grunted. Thirty was older, but not old. "What's his name?"

She thought abut lying, but she wasn't a liar and she knew eventually it would come back to bite her. "Storm," she said softly.

He stared at her, unblinking.

"No comment?" she asked.

"Is that his real name or one of those fancy artist names?"

"It's his real name."

He shook his head. "No, I don't have a comment. I don't believe in kicking a man while he's down, and with a name like that he's definitely down."

She tittered. "His sister's name is Sunshine."

"Now that's cute," he said. "I like that."

"You're a study in contrasts sometimes, Cameron." She closed her eyes again and tipped her face to the sun. He was still smiling over her girlish giggle when she closed her eyes. His smile remained while he studied her. He was almost overcome with the desire to kiss her, and it shocked him. This was *Belle*. Never in a million years would he have guessed he might someday be attracted to her, and yet he was, alarmingly so. Was he that lonely or was it something about her?

She felt his eyes on her and opened hers, not understanding the intensity of his gaze. Nervously, she looked forward.

"There's a foot coming out of that cow," she said, pointing to the cow in front of them.

He glanced at the cow and dashed his palm on the steering wheel. Then he began unbuttoning his shirt. Unlike the previous night, it was light enough to see exactly what she'd missed the previous evening, which was a lot, as it turned out. She watched, enraptured, as he took off his flannel shirt, opened the glove box, and took out a box of antibacterial wipes. He scrubbed his arms past his elbows like some sort of makeshift field surgeon, then walked to the cow and calmly stuck his hands inside it. He pushed the calf's foot inside. She saw the strain on his face as he manually turned the calf around inside its mother. The mother cow bellowed painfully. Belle winced at the thought of what she must be suffering.

Until that moment, Belle never would have guessed she would find the sight of a man with his hands in a cow attractive. But Cam had always been nice looking with his blondish brown hair, hazel eyes that were more green than brown, and of course the elusive dimple he hid from most of the world as if it were a shameful weakness to have one. The look on his face was both determined and confident, as if it never occurred to him that he might not succeed at whatever he tried. It was a look she knew well, one he almost always wore. And now there was his chest. *Yowza.* Years of working cattle had created a fine looking specimen in Cameron King. While Belle watched him work, she tried to think of ways to get her hands on his chest. For scientific purposes, really; she simply wanted to find out if it felt as solid as it looked.

He finished with his task and came back to the vehicle. While he used more antibacterial wipes to clean himself, they watched as the cow easily dropped her calf.

"Good job, Cam. You did it. That was amazing."

"Technically the cow did it," Cam said. To his horror, he felt himself blushing under her praise. He had been turning calves his whole life and no one had ever complimented him on it. It was nice, that little bit of recognition for a job well done.

He finished scrubbing his arms and picked up his shirt. After he stuffed his arms through the holes, she swatted his hands aside and began fastening his buttons for him. She didn't explain why, she simply locked her eyes on his chest and buttoned away. Not that he was complaining. It was an intimate thing, he realized, to have someone else dress him.

"Uh-oh," she said when she reached his stomach. I think I saw a tick. Hold still." She lifted his shirt and picked the tiny black bug off his abdomen, tossing it over the side of the vehicle. "I'd better make sure there aren't any more." She lifted his shirt again and began skimming her hands along his chest, stomach, and back. He had never seen anyone search for a tick so thoroughly using her fingers before, but maybe she didn't know how it was supposed to be done, citified as she was.

"I think you're all clear," she announced after a moment of careful searching. She finished buttoning his shirt and patted his chest a couple of times. "There you go." She patted his chest again. "All done."

After one more idiotic pat, Belle reluctantly ripped her hands away from him and turned to look out her side. *Note to self: don't touch his chest again. It feels even better than it looks.*

CHAPTER 8

He drove her to check on a few more cows, and then it started to rain. There was a hard plastic top on the cart, but it did nothing to stop the cold wind from cutting through her clothes. Because they were parked observing another cow, there was nowhere nearby to go to escape the weather. Instead, Cam put his arm around her, drawing her close to his sheltering warmth.

She rested her head on his shoulder and enjoyed the peaceful moment. Sometimes in New York, she missed the silence of Montana. There one of her three phones rang off the hook, her various computers beeped at her, cabbies yelled at her, horns honked, tires screeched along with eight million voices creating an endless cacophony of sound. Here the only noise was the sound of the rain pelting the plastic above her head. That, and Cam's deep, even breathing. She should have known it wouldn't last.

"Why didn't you dress for the weather?" Cam groused. He fastened his other arm around her, lacing his fingers together to create a kind of cage. "You're freezing."

"I dressed for the weather in New York. I don't own many parkas anymore." Their lips were by each other's ears, a necessity in order to talk and be heard above the rain.

"You look like a New York girl," he said. "What's it like there? Why do you love it so much?"

"Because it's not here," she answered without thinking.

He stiffened. "What's wrong with here?"

Everything," she said. As long as she had started down this road, she might as well be honest. "The weather, the cattle, the people, the lack of anything modern or cultured. The ignorance, the poverty…Do you really want me to go on?"

"No, I think you've said enough." His tone was clipped, but he didn't let her go. "You know what your problem is?" He didn't wait for her to try and answer before he continued. "You're a snob."

She wrenched away from him and looked up. "I am not a snob."

"You are. You think you're so much better than us because you've lived in the big city for four years."

"I do not." Maybe she did a little, but there was no way she would admit it. "You're as narrow-minded as the rest of them. You think everyone from the city is evil."

"I don't," he argued. "Layla's from Chicago and I never for a minute thought *she* was bad."

"Meaning that I am?" she asked defensively.

"You're not from the city. You *live* in the city. There's a big difference. No matter how far you run, you can't get away from your roots."

"Oh yes I can," she practically yelled, feeling a little desperate at his words. She was not a Montana girl; she was a New Yorker, sophisticated and cultured.

"Why would you want to?" He looked around and spread his hands. "This is Montana. It's the most beautiful, majestic place in the whole country. We have mountains and space and trees and wildlife. What do you have in the city but a bunch of buildings and noise?"

"How would you know? You've never been there. Try it sometime and you might like it," she challenged.

"Maybe I will," he said placidly, shocking her speechless. "You know my cousin lives in New York. She's been bugging us for years to visit."

"Which cousin?"

"Kelsey. I don't think you ever met her."

"No, I don't think so. I only remember Jason. Dreamy sigh."

He scowled. "What's so great about Jason?"

"What isn't? He was always so cool and manly."

"And what are the rest of us, ballet dancers?"

"No, it was something about him. What's he doing now?"

There was no way he would tell her Jason was now a federal marshal in Chicago, the same one who'd brought Layla to them as part of the Witness Protection Program. "He works, like every other person in my family."

"I thought you and Jason were close."

"We are. He still visits whenever he can."

"Then why do you sound so angry?"

"I'm not. Jason's great. He's *dreamy*."

She giggled again, softening him. He put his arm around her again, pulling her close. The rain petered out, but he made no move to let her go. She rested her head on his impressive chest, grateful for his encompassing warmth.

"The rain stopped," she commented sleepily.

"So it did," he said. His thumb eased up and down the graceful curve of her neck, soothing her as it skimmed softly behind her ear.

She smoothed her hand absently over his chest. "I don't suppose you have any more ticks on you."

"No," he said, puzzled by the question. "Why?"

"Never mind," she said.

Reluctantly, they separated and sat back. He drove back to the house in time for supper. "You're staying, right?"

She bit her lip uncertainly. Talking to Layla was her number one priority, but she felt the sudden need to distance herself from Cam. Then she glanced at his smug, familiar face and laughed at herself. This was Cameron King, same aggravating boy as ever; why would she need space from him?

"Sure, thanks," she said, turning calculating eyes toward the kitchen. "Maybe I can help Layla with supper."

"Layla prefers for us to stay out of her kitchen while she's working," Cam said.

"She didn't seem like the territorial type to me."

"That's because you don't know her. She's a tigress. Don't turn your back on her while she has a knife in her hand. Want me to carry you to the house?"

In answer, she jumped out of the ATV and darted up the porch steps, arriving breathless in the living room. Coy and Ivy turned to look at her with the same expression they had been using since she arrived yesterday. It was a combination of shock, wonder, and delight she didn't understand. Surely they weren't so hard up for visitors that her presence should cause this much excitement.

"Belle, you're here," Coy declared, surprised.

"Nothing gets by you," Cam said, stepping into the room behind her and resting his hand—possessively?—on her waist.

"Were you guys together all day?" Coy asked, staring at his brother's hand where it rested on Belle's waist. Did he know he was touching Belle Landry like that? Was he aware of the way chemistry now popped and crackled between them?

"Cam turned a calf," Belle blurted excitedly, then realized it was something that probably happened on a daily basis here. "I haven't seen that since I left Manhattan a few days ago," she added, much more subdued.

Ivy chuckled. "You're funny, Belle."

"Don't encourage her," Cam said. "She's already too big for her britches."

"According to my personal trainer, my britches fit perfectly," she said, head tilted defiantly in his direction.

He stuck his finger in her belt loop and tugged. "Hmm. What do you know? He's right."

"Wow," Coy whispered the word as if he couldn't stop himself.

"Why does he keep saying that?" Belle asked.

"He's amazed at the changes in you," Cam answered with a wry smile.

"Yes, that's why I'm amazed," Coy said sarcastically, making fleeting eye contact with his twin.

"Dinner," Layla called.

The family migrated to the kitchen, appearing en masse as if they'd been summoned, which they had.

"This is amazing," Belle said when she saw the spread Layla had prepared. "Where did you learn to cook?"

"Here," Layla answered.

"Shorty taught her," Cade added.

"Shorty's still alive?" Belle blurted.

"Not anymore," Cam sad sadly. "Rest his soul." Reverently, he pressed his hand over his heart.

Belle's eyes squeezed shut. "I can't believe I keep saying stuff like that."

Layla laughed. "Shorty is alive and well, Belle. Cam's teasing you."

"Are you ever serious?" Belle asked him, not understanding why the rest of the family cracked up laughing.

"Only occasionally," Cam said, his eyes twinkling at her.

She returned her attention to Layla. "You could cater. Your presentation is perfect, and the taste is wonderful."

Layla flushed. "Thank you. There's not much use for caterers around here, though."

"You could find work if you set your mind to it. You can do anything, be anything. What are your interests?"

"That's the problem," Layla said. "I don't know. I have a lot of interests."

"Like what?" Belle leaned forward expectantly, head perched in her hand.

"Do you want her resume?" Cam asked, annoyed.

"I'm making conversation," Belle snapped, using her free hand to shove his leg. Not that it did much good, sculpted as they were from solid granite, apparently. Were there any ticks hiding there? Maybe she should check later…

"We should play a game after supper," Ivy said diplomatically, drawing Belle's intense gaze from Cam's legs.

Coy dropped his head in his hands with a groan. "Sweetheart, you have no idea what you've unleashed on us all."

Belle and Cam shared a conspiratorial smile. "A game sounds good," Cam said. "I have exactly the one in mind."

"Of course you do," Coy said.

After supper, Cam disappeared into the den to retrieve the game.

"I didn't know we had trivial pursuit," Layla said. "I've never seen it before."

"That's because I thought I burned it after last time," Coy said. "Like *Jumanji*."

"What's the big deal?" Layla asked.

"You'll see," Coy said cryptically. "We'll all be on a team against Belle and Cam. They'll play individually."

"That doesn't seem fair," Ivy said.

"It's not," Coy said. "We'll still lose. Take my word."

"He's right," Cade added. "But at least it will be over quickly and we can all move on with our lives. Well, some of us can." He eyed Cam and Belle.

Supper was cleared, the game was set up, and Ivy, Layla, and Josh began to understand what Coy had been talking about. The competition between Cam and Belle was cutthroat. Finally, they were the only two who had all their pie pieces and they had to select each other's final questions. When it was Belle's turn, Cam chose a sports question, and she missed it.

"Sports are still your Achilles heel, huh?" he taunted.

When it was her turn to choose for him, she selected a pop culture question. He pretended to agonize over her selection but answered correctly, winning the game. Then he remained suspiciously quiet while she said her goodbyes to the rest of the family.

The silence continued as he walked her to her car. "Get it over with," she commanded when she couldn't take it anymore.

"I was trying to remember if you've ever beaten me at that game." He touched his finger to his chin, pretending to muse. "I can't remember. Have you?"

"You know I haven't," she said tersely. "Since when are you so well-versed in pop culture?"

"Since two girls moved into the house," he said.

"At least I still have the swimming competition in my corner," she said.

"So you say," he said.

She was alerted by his aggravatingly cocky tone. "What's that supposed to mean?"

He leaned close and whispered in her ear. "It means four years ago, I let you win." With that, he turned and walked back toward the house.

She took a running leap and jumped on his back, cinching her arm around his neck and pulling backward to cut off his air supply. "You take that back, Cameron King. I beat you fair and square."

He walked backwards until she was pressed against her car, relieving the pressure on his neck. Then he turned to face her. "Make me," he whispered. Her arm was still around his neck, drawing him so close their faces were almost touching.

There was a breathless moment when she thought he might kiss her, and a confusing moment when she hoped he would. But before she could find out, she spoke.

"I should go."

"You think so?" he asked, eyes still on her lips.

"I'm pretty sure," she said, tone uncertain.

"It's your call, Isabelle."

She paused, uncertain again. His finger trailed down her cheek, making her decision harder. But, as ever, rational thought eventually prevailed. "I'm going to go."

He released her. She toppled back against her car and fumbled for the handle, scooting her body toward her door without taking her eyes off him.

"Come back tomorrow," he said, and it wasn't a request.

"I have to work tomorrow."

"You can work here. I'll share my office."

"I'll think about it," she said. Finally, her numb fingers brushed the handle and clutched at it like it was a lifeline. After a few failed attempts, she opened the door and practically fell inside, speeding off down the long driveway without another word.

For the second night in a row, Cam stood staring after her and scratching his head at the unexpected turn of events.

CHAPTER 9

The next morning Belle arrived at the ranch office bright and early. At least it was early to her; Cam had been up for hours. He opened the door at her knock and scanned her up and down, secretly enjoying the sight of her in her gray tailored suit and tortoiseshell glasses. There was something about smart girls that got him every time, and especially this smart girl, apparently.

"I thought you got contacts," he said.

"These are for reading."

He nodded and opened the door wider, admitting her entrance. She had the strange feeling she had been granted acceptance into some exclusive boys' only clubhouse.

"It looks different than I remember," she said. Last time she had been here, their father ran the place. It was one large room with a desk and phone. Now the large space had been divided into three enclosed offices. There was a copier, fax machine, phones with more than one line, and a few modern-looking computers.

"Hey, Belle," Cade's voice floated from one of the offices. Belle followed the sound and paused in the doorway.

"Hey, Cade."

"Cade does all the accounting and financial paperwork, freeing me up to do other things," Cam informed her. "He's been a lifesaver."

"Am I blushing?" Cade asked.

"No, but I think I see a few tears glimmering in those eyes," Cam said. "My office is this way." He led Belle down the hall a few paces and opened the door for her. It was a simple office and also equipped with new-looking modern equipment.

"You've really brought it into the twenty first century," she said.

"I've been busy bringing the entire ranch up to speed. Everything is computerized now. Each cow has a virtual identity to keep track of parentage, immunizations, growth, and etcetera."

"Don't you have a million cows or something? I can't imagine how much time that must take."

"Don't try. It's insane. I need a secretary, but people aren't exactly beating down my door to work in the middle of nowhere." He eyed her speculatively. "Although, you're here now..." He trailed off, letting his meaning hang.

She adjusted her glasses and gave him an imperious look. "Don't get any ideas. I have two secretaries myself. Although, I might suggest that you have a girl in your house who is looking for a project."

His face lit. "I never thought of Layla. That's a good idea."

"Do you have wi-fi?" she asked.

"Yes. Plug in anywhere if you don't want to waste your battery." He waved his hand to the comfortable looking leather loveseat sitting against one wall before sitting behind his desk.

"Do you mind if I have my secretary transfer my calls here for today?" she asked.

"No. We have a seldom-used line. Here's the number."

"Thank you." She paused again. "I'm going to need to call him a few times. Is that okay? I can pay you."

"I think we can afford a buck fifty for your calls. Besides, we have a bundle deal with unlimited long distance."

"Thank you. I appreciate it. This is a much better setup than my parents' house, or even dad's store. I think you may be the only person in town with a high speed internet connection."

He smiled, watching her as she set up her temporary workstation. Was that the reason she had come back today? And, if so, was it the only one? He tried to concentrate on his work, but he was continually distracted by watching her. *So efficient. So adorable.* She selected the appropriate line and called her secretary. He shouldn't have been surprised her secretary was a man, but he still was.

Angrily, she clicked on an email and punched another number into the telephone. This time she used the cordless phone and began pacing the room. "Hi, Sue. This is Belle Landry. I need to speak with Joel, please. No, I would prefer not to wait. It's important, and I think he'll take my call. Yes, thank you." There was a short pause while she tapped her foot impatiently.

"Hi, Joel, it's Belle."

Cam sat back and laced his fingers behind his head, all pretense of concentration on his own work was gone at Belle's cool and professional tone. He had no idea who Joel was, but he suddenly felt sorry for him because he was about to lose.

"When we spoke last week, our deal was for a one nine. I read your copy of the contract, and it reads one seventy five. That's unacceptable, Joel." Her eyes narrowed and her lips pressed into a thin line while she listened to whatever Joel had to say.

"No. Absolutely not. I didn't want to have to play hardball as long as you were being reasonable, but I have to tell you Simon and Shuster is on the line for two. My client wanted to go with you because he's loyal, but if I point out to him that you're about to go back on your word, I think he'll see things differently. Yes. Yes. Yes. Okay. Send me the amended contract today. If everything is in order, I'll have it couriered to my client this afternoon. You too. Goodbye, Joel." She pushed the button to end the call, only then realizing that she was perched on the edge of Cam's desk, facing him.

"Sorry," she said. She started to hop off the edge of the desk, but he rested his hand on her leg.

"Can I assume those were millions of dollars you were talking about?"

"Yes."

"And what is your commission?"

"Fifteen percent."

"So you made fifteen percent of almost two million dollars."

"Yes."

"This wasn't the first time, huh?"

"No. I deal with big clients and big numbers."

"And you're very good," he presumed.

She shrugged and grinned at him, suddenly cocky. "That's the rumor in Manhattan."

He wasn't surprised, exactly, but he was a little taken aback by seeing her work in person. She was a force to be reckoned with. Some men might be intimidated by her. He was not.

She noted his hand was still on her knee, his thumb making absent circles. When they made eye contact, he smiled. She leaned slightly forward and returned his smile. The phone rang and she lunged for it.

"King Ranch, this is Belle speaking. How may I direct your call? Oh, Mrs. King. Yes, ma'am, it's Belle Landry. Yes, ma'am, and you? Yes, he's right here." Cam reached for the phone, but Belle leaned away from him. "Yes, we've been getting reacquainted. Behaving? Not hardly. Right now he's touching my knee, *with intention*, and a couple of days ago, while shirtless, he said he…"

Cam lunged for the phone and plucked it from her grasp. "Mom, I can explain," he said desperately.

"If you'd like to make a call, please hang up and try your call again…" the automated voice said.

"Gotcha," Belle said.

Cam hung up the phone, clasped her ankles, and dragged her toward him. Before she could reach him, the phone rang—her line—and, breathless now, she reached for it.

"Belle Landry."

He knew by her caught, guilty expression it was her boyfriend. She hopped off the desk and paced to the opposite side of the room.

"How's Montana?" Storm asked.

"Good. Things are good," she said.

"Did you sign your author yet?"

She blew out a breath. "No. There are complications." It was difficult not to look at Cam when she said "complications."

"I was hoping you would be done already. I miss you, Belle. There's no one here to tell me what to do."

"I don't tell you what to do," she said defensively. Behind her, Cameron snorted his amusement. She glared at him. *Stop eavesdropping,* she mouthed.

Make me, he mouthed in return and she got caught up staring at his lips, so full, so pretty.

"I meant that in a good way," Storm continued, snapping her attention back to him. "You help order my life. I can't think straight when you're not here." He paused. "I think when you come home we need to talk."

Her first odd reaction to that statement had been to think, *Home? I am home.* Out loud she said, "About what?"

"About taking the next step in our relationship."

"Now isn't a good time, Storm. I'm busy at work."

"You're always busy at work. I'm beginning to realize that's never going to change."

"I'm only twenty two," she pointed out.

"You don't act like it. You act older than me. If there's anyone in the world mature enough to handle commitment, it's you, Belle. But I can tell you're freaking out. We'll wait until you get home. Think about it, okay? We could work, I know we could."

"I'll think about it," she said hesitantly.

"That's all I ask. I'll talk to you soon, Babe. Bye."

"Bye."

She hung up the phone and stared dazedly at a picture of a wolf. "Who painted this?"

"My mother. How's Storm?"

"He's swell."

"He wants to get serious, huh?"

"How can you tell?" she asked.

"Because you're about to run screaming from the room."

"How do you know? You can't see my face." She still had her back to him, staring unblinkingly at the badly painted wolf. One of its paws was three times the size of the other paws and one fang hung down below his mouth like a saber tooth. Some part of her brain acknowledged that it was vaguely soothing to learn his mother wasn't perfect. At least she had one flaw; she was a horrible artist.

"I just know. And since I figure the only thing that terrifies you is getting serious with a man you don't love, I put two and two together."

"Who says I don't love him?" Tearing her eyes from the misshapen wolf wasn't easy, but somehow she managed to face him.

"Do you?"

Did she love Storm? She had been infatuated with him and flattered by his interest in her. He was handsome and popular, sort of a grown up version of a high school superstar. Only in the grown up version, talent and personality mattered more than looks or whatever other elusive element made one kid popular over another.

"I don't know. What is love? If it's mutual like and respect then, yes, I love him."

"What about chemistry?" he asked.

"I aced it both in high school and in college."

"I remember, but that wasn't what I was talking about and you know it."

"Define chemistry," she requested.

He stood and came around his desk, then took her hand and drew her close before perching on the edge of the desk. "I think chemistry is what happens when two people are attracted to each other despite the fact that they can't get along. Or maybe because of it." He studied her hand while he talked, tracing it with his index finger, and then he finally looked up at her. "Wouldn't you agree?"

She tugged her hand free and used it to smooth down her already glassy hair. "I wouldn't know. I haven't had much experience with this sort of thing."

"Want to do a little experiment?"

"Huh?"

"An experiment. You aced chemistry. Don't tell me you don't know what an experiment is."

"I'm familiar with the term, but not its usage in this context."

"Have you kissed your boyfriend? I mean, I assume so, but who knows how things happen in the city."

The abrupt and nosy question caught her off guard, causing her to answer honestly. "Yes." If she had been paying attention, she would have told him it was none of his business, as well as where to get off.

"How was it?"

"None of your business."

"That bad?" he asked.

She scowled.

"The point is I think you need to have a wide range of comparison. What if you think you have chemistry with him, but you don't? You could be making a big mistake with him."

"I don't see what this has to do with you," she said, although she knew all too well where he was going with this and had no plan to be a part of it.

"As one of your oldest friends, I feel honor bound to help you out by offering my services," he said. Sometime during his speech, his hands snaked to her waist and drew her close. Of course she planned to stop him; she simply wanted to see how far he planned to go with things so she would know exactly what type of lecture he was due for. And, because she was so close to him, it was only natural that she rest her palms on his magnificent chest. Were there ticks in this office? She hoped so.

"What did you have in mind?"

He drew her impossibly closer and rested his lips on her ear so when he spoke, his lips lightly caressed her earlobe. Shivers ran from that ear all the way down to her ankles. She gripped his shirt, holding herself aloft with effort as she tried not to drape herself on him. "We have two dozen cowboys on this ranch, and they're all single. You can kiss every one of them if you want."

CHAPTER 10

*B*elle's first reaction was fury because she had walked right into his immature trap. But she was much too competitive to let her irritation show. Instead, she smiled, though she now found it easier to stand and her shivers had magically dried up. She pressed her lips to his ear and spoke softly, taking note of the fact that now he was the one who seemed a little weak in the knees. "That's awfully generous of you, Cameron, but I have some limitations. Any cowboy I kiss has to be clean, well groomed, polite, and approximately my age. Don't try to pawn me off on someone like Shorty who is probably ninety and has none of the teeth he was born with."

He pulled back to study her, trying to calculate his next move. "All right. I'll go see who is in the barn. A lot of our hands fit your description, and I'll even let you have the final say." He smirked at her, sure she would back down. He should have known she'd rather die first.

"That's sweet. What a good friend you are. Let's go now while my breath is still minty fresh." She preceded him out of the office and had to wait outside a few seconds while he caught up with her. "What took you so long? Are you having second thoughts?"

"No, I took a minute to call ahead and have them ready. Come on." Clasping her hand, he led her at a trot behind him.

Her insides clenched with anxiety. She wasn't one of those women who could kiss a man and not have it mean anything. In her lifetime, she had kissed fewer people than she could count on one hand. On the other hand, neither was she one of those women who could easily lose a battle. Especially not to Cameron King. Whatever it took, she wouldn't back down. He would break first, or she would kiss every cowboy on this ranch, toothless and tobacco stained or not.

"Here we are," Cam said. He drew her up short by placing his arm around her shoulders. Before her stood what looked like a hastily assembled cowboy army. A dozen smirking ranch hands stood at attention in a semi-straight line, darting glances at her and trying desperately not to laugh.

The sight of them was daunting. Some of them barely looked old enough to shave. Cam smirked along with them, sure she would cave. But she shrugged away from him, clasped her hands behind her back, and began to prowl back in forth in front of them, inspecting them.

"If any of you uses tobacco products, raise your hand," she commanded.

Three of them men raised their hands.

"Thank you for your honesty. Step back please." She waited while the three tobacco users stepped back before she turned to look at Cam. "These will do. Thank you for your help. You may leave now." She made an imperious, dismissive gesture with her hand, shooing him toward the door.

"No way. These are my men and I don't trust you. I'm staying right here until this is over." He crossed his arms and leaned casually against the barn door.

"Suit yourself," she said easily. Calling upon her acting skills, she suppressed her nervousness and walked confidently to the first cowboy in line. He was tall and strapping, as they all were, and she began to think this might not be the traumatic ordeal she'd envisioned. Grasping his chin between her thumb and forefinger, she turned his face back and forth slightly, studying him.

"What's your name, cowboy?"

"Tanner," he said.

"How old are you, Tanner?"

"Twenty five."

"Do you have a girlfriend?"

"No, but if this goes well I have high hopes."

She laughed. "I like an optimist. Thank you for helping me out with this."

"The pleasure is all mine."

"Cam thinks I need to learn a few things, so don't hold back. Do your best."

"I'll give it everything I've got," Tanner promised. He rested his hands on Belle's waist, drawing her slightly closer. She closed her eyes, tipped her face up, and waited. Nothing happened. After a second of nothingness, she opened her eyes and saw Tanner sprawled on his backside, Cam towering over him, fists clenched in anger.

"What are you doing?" she yelled, hands on hips. "Are you crazy?"

"Apparently." He helped Tanner to his feet. "Add another personal day to your schedule, and take yourself out on my dime."

"Sure thing, Boss," Tanner said. He didn't seem upset by the ruckus, but Belle was horrified and unwilling to let it go. Cam, sensing as much, grabbed her wrist and dragged her behind him out of the barn.

"You…" she started, but he cut her off.

"Save it. Not in front of the men."

He was insane. He could drag her into a line up of men waiting to kiss her, knock one of them over for touching her, then drag her back out again, but she wasn't allowed to talk about it in front of them?

"If you think I'm going to do what you tell me, then you have greatly misjudged me."

His response was to once again pick her up and throw her over his shoulder. This time he pinned her legs to his chest so she couldn't kick him. They reached the old farm truck. He tossed her inside, drove to a remote spot on the ranch, and turned the truck off.

"Are you crazy?"

Neither of them knew who yelled it first because they erupted at the same time.

"You were going to kiss all of them to avoid losing face. That's not normal behavior, Isabelle."

"Oh, and rounding up your employees to kiss a strange woman is perfectly natural, Cameron," she yelled.

"I thought you would give up before you did something so idiotic. I should have known better."

"Yes, you should have. I don't lose, Cam. Ever. Not when we were kids, not when we're adults. I don't give up and I don't back down. This is who I am. This is who I'll always be."

She crossed her arms over her chest and awaited his sizzling reply, but he had none to give. He sat staring at her, processing all she had said, all that had happened. And he came to a sudden realization about himself. He would have been disappointed in her if she backed down from the challenge. One of the things that made Belle so very Belle was her indomitable, unstoppable personality. Any other woman probably would have slapped him for teasing her into thinking he was going to kiss her. At the very least, they would have balked when he mentioned the possibility of kissing all his cowboys. Not Belle. She had gamely met him play for play, turning up the heat to the boiling point and then waiting for him to crack.

And most surprising of all was the fact that he *had* cracked. Until today, he had never laid a hand on any of his employees before. But for some reason the sight of Tanner closing his eyes and leaning toward Belle with obvious intent had snapped the control Cam had worked all his life to achieve. And he had lost. To Belle. Again. In all his life, she was the only person who had ever beaten him at anything, the only woman who had ever stood up to him and told him to take a hike.

Turning away from her to face front, he started the car and headed back toward the ranch.

"Cam, are you that mad?" Belle asked nervously. "You've never gone silent before."

"I'm not mad," he assured her quietly. Instead, he was scared out of his mind. He needed to get back to his office, review his written list, and remember Belle wasn't on it. She wasn't the girl for him. She lived in New York. She scared the living daylights out of most people who had half a brain. She made him crazy. She couldn't ride a horse. She made him crazy. She hated Montana. She made him crazy. If she was any indication, insanity ran thick in her family. And, most importantly, *she made him crazy*. Really, really crazy. So crazy, in fact, that he hadn't been able to sleep a full night since she arrived. So crazy he couldn't get her off his mind. So crazy he had physically attacked one of his most faithful employees for fulfilling the insane order that he himself had given.

The truck jerked to a halt in front of the house. Belle looked between him and the house, the wheels in her head always turning. "I guess I can go visit with Layla for a while."

"No," Cam blurted, white knuckling the steering wheel. He ran his hands over his face and tried to think. She had him between a rock and a hard place. He couldn't let her spend time with Layla, but he couldn't afford to spend any more time with her himself for fear of what might become of him. Weighing his options, he tried to decide which was the lesser of two evils. At last he gave a prolonged sigh and rested his head on the steering wheel.

"Go out with me tonight," he said resignedly.

"Where?" she asked.

"You choose."

She didn't even have to pause. It was as if she had a read answer when there was no way she could have, but that was Belle, never without a backup plan. "The city. We'll take the train. Pick me up in an hour and a half and wear a suit." With that, she let herself out of the truck, hopped into her car, and sped toward home.

He stared after her, wondering how it was possible that she came up with a plan for tonight so quickly. Had she known he was going to ask her to go out and then allow her to choose? No. That wasn't possible. It was simply Belle's way to conjure an intricate plan on the spur of the moment. No doubt it would be some grand evening with multiple activities. And no doubt he would hate every minute of it.

Once again, he rested his head on the steering wheel with a weary chuckle. No doubt about it, the woman made him crazy and he was in very big trouble.

CHAPTER 11

Exactly an hour and a half later, Cam showed up on the Landry's doorstep, as nervous as he had been for his first ever date. He smoothed his hand over his already immaculate hair, glad for the crew cut that kept his curls under control. No one would ever take him seriously if his hair was as curly as Coy's, which it would be if he ever let it grow past a quarter of an inch. He knocked on the door unsmiling, wondering if Belle's parents would answer and grill him the way some of his teenage crushes' parents had done.

But they didn't. Belle answered the door herself and Cam stared at her, speechless with surprise at the unexpected sight of her. Over and over he had to keep reminding himself she was pretty now. In his mind she was forever the knobby-kneed little bookworm of their youth. Oddly, he rather liked thinking of her that way. It comforted him that he was attracted to *her* and not her new, polished appearance.

But now as he swept his gaze from head to foot and back up again, all thoughts of her personality vanished. She was beautiful in a steel gray silk dress that draped gracefully from her neck to her ankles. Her high heels made her come up to his nose instead of to his chin like normal.

"Ready?" she asked cheerfully. Apparently she wasn't as affected by the sight of him in a suit as he was of her in a dress.

"Shouldn't I say hello to your parents?" he asked.

"No. Dad's at the store, of course, and mom is there, too. April is approaching, and she does all his taxes, which is kind of a feat, really. It's not easy to be an employer and do taxes."

"Tell me about it. I wanted to throw a party when Cade started doing ours."

"He takes a lot of weight off your shoulders," she guessed.

"He does. I would never have wished for the accident to happen, but he's made the best of what he has to work with. He's invaluable to me now, thanks to Layla." He told her how depressed Cade had been when Layla came to live with them and how Layla had drawn him out of his shell, showing him how to live again with his new disability.

"So it sounds like it's his turn to be supportive of her dream," Belle mused.

"Of course he's supportive. He loves her."

"Even if it means she might have to leave the ranch in order to follow her dream?"

"Why would she have to leave? She loves the ranch; it's her home."

Belle shrugged. There was no reason Layla wouldn't be able to write from Montana, but maybe she didn't want to. She couldn't help feeling like everyone wanted Layla to stay for their own reasons, not taking into account what was best for her.

"But do you think Cade would be willing to go with her if she chose to leave?"

He frowned, thinking about it. "No. None of us would ever leave the ranch for any reason. It's our heritage. It's in our blood. Multiple generations of Kings have worked hard to provide for us. We can't turn our backs on that for the sake of some woman."

"I suppose," Belle agreed. "Plus, I don't really believe someone should have to give up so much of him or herself for someone else. I am who I am, and I won't change or compromise for any man." She finished speaking with a resolute nod of her head.

"That sentiment will be really comforting when you die alone," he said.

Now it was her turn to frown. "Why should I? Why can't it be that way?"

"Because you want someone to live in your world and follow your rules. Either he'll resent you, or you'll turn into his mother," Cam said.

She was uncomfortable with his assessment, especially because it already resembled her life. Storm liked to be taken care of, and he liked for Belle to be the one to do it. After becoming frustrated with his schizophrenic financial situation, she had automated all his bills and put him on a budget. Now he called her for advice on every decision he had to make. At first, she had enjoyed the feeling of control and power it gave her, but now she was becoming bored with it. After a few years, she knew she would come to resent him for his dependence on her. But where could she find a man who wouldn't capitulate to her strong personality without losing herself completely?

Cam waited for her to walk down the porch steps in front of him. When she reached the bottom and realized he hadn't moved, she turned back to face him. He stared at her, his face pinched and lacking color.

"What's wrong?" she asked, concerned. Had he suddenly developed the flu? If the sheen of sweat on his brow was any indication, the answer was yes.

"Your dress is…There's no…It's gone."

It took her a second to realize what she was talking about, and then the wind on her back reminded her. While the material in the front came up to her neck, it swooped low in the back, skimming her tailbone.

"You're looking at me like you've never seen a dress before," she said.

"Not like that," he said. "It's, ah, very nice."

She blinked at him in astonishment. Was he staring at her with that gleam in his eye because he was *attracted* to her? "Why are you looking at me like that?" she demanded, hands on hips.

"Why not?" he said with a slow smile, once again his cocky self.

"Isn't that the point of the dress?"

She had never thought about it before. There were probably some women who dressed with the sole intent of attracting a man's attention, but Belle had never been one of them. She wore what she liked. When she saw this dress in a boutique, she had thought it was pretty. But now, seeing the affect it was having on Cam, she was glad she had bought it.

"Behave," she admonished, purposely turning her back to him while she waited for him to open her car door.

"I could say the same thing to you," he said. His palm rested lightly on her back as he helped her into the tall truck. A tingling sensation remained when he pulled it away. It was only a few blocks to the train station, but she was glad he drove. Her feet already hurt. Why wasn't it possible to make a pretty shoe that was also comfortable?

He paid for their tickets and rested his palm on her back again while he helped her find a seat. "So where are we going?" he asked when they were seated.

"You choose the restaurant," she said.

"That's magnanimous of you," he said dryly.

"I was intending on paying."

"Over my dead body," he said, horrified at the very idea of a woman paying for him.

She rolled her eyes. "It's the twenty first century. I'm the one who arranged this date. It's only fair I pay."

"No way. Confine your feminism to New York, please. This is Montana."

She made a show of looking out the train window at the flat landscape. "Really? Thank you for pointing that out to me. The bustling crowds and towering skyscrapers confused me for a minute."

"Have you always been this sarcastic? I can't remember," he said.

"'Sarcasm is the last refuge of modest and chaste-souled people when the privacy of their soul is coarsely and intrusively invaded,'" she quoted.

"And now you're quoting Dostoevsky. Are you trying to impress me?"

"No." But she was impressed he knew the quote was Dostoevsky. He had always been intelligent, but she hadn't taken him for a reader.

Guessing her thoughts, he gave her a wry smile. "An occasional book makes its way to Montana. Next year we're hoping to get talkies at the moving picture theater."

"The town has a moving picture theater now?" she countered.

He laughed. "You have a comeback for everything, don't you, Belle?"

"Yes."

"That's why it's all the more disconcerting I like you," Cam said. "By all rights, you should get on my nerves. But instead you make me laugh. Kind of a lot. You take me outside of myself, make me think of fun and adventure in a way no one else ever has. And you're so pretty, Belle. So very pretty."

She was unprepared for him to say something sweet. And then to her further befuddlement he clasped her hand, brought it to his lips, and kissed it. When she realized she was staring at him mouth agape, she snapped her jaw shut. For once she was speechless. And no one else had ever left her without words before.

Cam had the same realization. He smiled, enjoying the small moment of triumph. Seemingly he had done the impossible; he had shut her up. Her silence continued as the train jerked to a halt. He kept her hand and used it to lead her behind him and out of the train. Once they were on solid ground, he dropped her hand and rested his palm on her back, guiding her toward the restaurant.

Belle hadn't been paying attention as he led her down the street. Absently, she had been studying the town and noting the changes. The city was slightly larger than their small town, and therefore the changes were more significant. For that reason when a familiar scent hit her nose, she looked up at the restaurant in surprise because the scent belonged in Manhattan, not Montana.

"Thai?" she asked, unable to trust her senses. Thai, in Montana. Maybe the apocalypse would happen now, all the signs were there: Belle had been rendered speechless by a man and ethnic food had arrived in Montana.

"Thai," Cam repeated, pleased with himself that he had once again surprised her.

She rested her hand on his bicep. "This is sweet, but you don't have to do this for me."

"I'm not," he said. "I have all the beef and potatoes I want on the ranch. Sometimes change is nice. I *like* Thai food. I eat here whenever I come to the city."

If he was purposely trying to impress her, he was succeeding, although why he should try was beyond her. They had known each other since kindergarten. There wasn't much left to discover about each other. Or was there? Either he had changed in the last four years, or she had never really known him. Whatever the reason, he was full of surprises tonight.

They ordered their food and sat at a small booth in the back. The restaurant was small, not fancy, and empty. Most of their business appeared to be carry out, if the number of people coming in and out was any indication.

"How did you find this place?" she asked.

"Last year I flew to Wyoming to look at a bull and when I returned I got snowed in. I stayed at a hotel down the street and found this place. Contrary to popular belief, I like to try new things."

"Were you alone, or did one of your brothers go with you?" she asked.

"I was alone."

For some reason, the thought of him snowed in all by himself and eating here alone made her sad. "Did you get lonely?"

He opened his mouth to tell her no, but hesitated. "A little," he admitted, tone sheepish.

"I would have gone with you," she declared impulsively. "I like to travel and try new food, too. My schedule doesn't leave a lot of room for travel, though. This is the first time I've left New York in four years and the first time I've taken a day off work."

"What did you do for Christmas all those years?" he asked. Their food was delivered to the table. They spent a moment arranging it before she answered.

"Once my parents came out to visit," she said.

"And the other three years?"

She stared hard at her food. "I was alone." Her soft tone matched his earlier one. She picked up her chopsticks, noting as she did so that he reached for his fork. He smiled when he noticed her stare, endearingly embarrassed.

"I've never been able to get the hang of those."

Using chopsticks wasn't an inherent skill; it was learned. Some of her Manhattan friends showed her because she was bumbling around, dropping them every other bite. "Try it like this." She reached across the table and positioned the sticks correctly in his fingers. "Pinch the top stick. Make sure the ends are even. Wedge the other stick there. It takes practice," she added when he dropped the bottom stick. She smiled as she watched him clamp his tongue between his teeth and try again until he got it right. Somehow the expression was familiar. Until she saw it, she didn't realize it was one she knew from school, his heavy-duty concentration face. How many times had she glanced across a classroom and saw Cameron King look like that? Too many to count.

"Thanks," he said, scooping a bit of sticky rice from his container. He held it out to her and she ate it. Likewise, she held out one of her spring rolls to him.

Over the remainder of dinner, they shared their food and talked about books they had read and movies they enjoyed. Surprisingly to both of them, they had similar tastes in both movies and books.

"Where to now?" Cam asked when they were finished.

"Spring Street," she answered.

He quirked an eyebrow at her. There wasn't much located on Spring Street, merely some old warehouses that had been renovated to house modern businesses. Downtown was small enough that everywhere was in walking distance, but since her feet already ached she wasn't looking forward to the journey. However, because this evening had been her idea, as had the shoes, she kept her complaints to herself.

Their combined hands bumped her hip as they walked, and only then did she realize she was holding hands with him. The sight baffled her. When and how had that happened? Had he taken her hand, or had she taken his? And why hadn't she noticed it to begin with?

"Here we are," she announced when they reached their destination, glad for a distraction from her tangled thoughts. As she expected, Cam looked around questioningly.

"Where are we? What is this place?"

"You'll see, my friend. Oh, you'll see." Now she was glad they were holding hands because she was able to lead him behind her. They stepped through the nondescript entryway and into a grand ballroom where several couples were already on the floor.

"You brought me dancing," he said, incredulous, resisting the urge to do a double take or rub his eyes. The outside was so nondescript and decrepit, he would never have guessed it could look so grand on the inside. Overhead a massive crystal chandelier sparkled and each wall was hung with swags of rich, blue fabric.

"I saw a flyer in my parents' paper for this charity fundraiser, and I thought it sounded like fun." She paused, taking in his flabbergasted expression. "But if you'd rather not..." She trailed off, trying to hide her disappointment.

"No, this is fine. I'm surprised. I figured you would drag me somewhere boring, like a lecture on gender studies or the anti-patriarchal merits of growing out your leg hair. I like dancing."

"I know," she said.

He turned to regard her, warming her from the inside with his intense inspection. "How do you know?"

"I saw you at homecoming in tenth grade. All the other boys looked like someone had pulled their teeth to get them on the dance floor, but not you. I could tell you were having fun. And I could tell you knew what you were doing."

"How could you tell?" He tried to picture himself laughing and smiling and couldn't conjure the image. He had always been reserved with his emotions.

She shook their joined hands between them, smiling a little. "You had the same look you used to get whenever you beat me on a test."

He laughed as he took out his wallet and made the contribution that would allow them entrance into the dance. "Who did you go to homecoming with that year? My memory is a blank."

"I didn't," she said. "I was on the decorating committee. That cow Cindy Parker and I disagreed over the decorations. She thought she won, but I showed her. I sneaked in a couple hours before the dance and redid everything. I was finishing up when everyone arrived."

He would have laughed at the vision of her single-handedly redecorating the gym if not for the other, sadder vision that crowded out the image. He remembered her as she had been in high school—an oddball outcast with no friends save Coy, standing in the shadows and watching everyone else have fun.

"You could have gone with us," he said. "Coy and I didn't have dates that year. We would have danced with you."

She let go of his hand in order to link her arm through his and give it a squeeze. "That's retroactively sweet of you, thank you. But high school was a long time ago, and I was never the type to let complete and total ostracism get me down."

High school was a long time ago, but he wasn't sure the other part of her statement was true. No one, no matter how strong, liked to be always on the outside looking in.

He squeezed her arm in return. "Well, you showed everyone. You went off and got pretty, rich, and successful in New York."

"And yet here I am at another dance in Montana," she said slowly, her eyes drifting toward the dancing couples. "Back to where I started."

"Not exactly, Belle. This time you have a date, and not only are you going to dance every dance, but they're all going to be with me. Other men are eyeing you like they're queuing up to take a turn. Don't make me punch a stranger at a charity ball."

She thought he was kidding but, remembering his earlier altercation with Tanner, she shifted slightly closer, resting her hand reassuringly on his impressive bicep. "For tonight, I'm all yours."

"Isabelle Landry, that might be the best news I've ever heard," he said, and then they danced.

CHAPTER 12

True to Cam's word, they danced every dance together, every single one, until they were breathless from laughter, breathless from spinning, breathless from everything. While it had been a delight to dance so much, Belle's feet were throbbing. When the dance ended, she tried to obscure her misery and failed horribly.

"What's wrong? Thai food not sitting well?" Cam asked.

"No, it's my feet. I think you broke them."

He glanced down at her feet, tipping his head to make his inspection. "I think it's those itty bitty stilts you've been trying to balance on." They exited the building and he stopped short in front of her. "Hop on, I'll carry you."

She didn't even think about protesting. What was the point of being friends with a strapping buck, if not to use him as a pack mule occasionally? "There's a reason people love cowboys," she said before hopping on his back.

He laughed. "And what's the reason?"

"They're strong, capable, chivalrous, proud, honorable, handsome, generous, surprising, funny." At some point she had switched from speaking about cowboys in general to him specifically, and she broke off abruptly, realizing her blunder. "Or so some believe," she added hastily, glad he couldn't see her flushed cheeks. "Those who have never met a cowboy might think those things." Great, now she was babbling.

"And what do those who have met a cowboy think?" he asked.

She studied the ground from her new, advanced height on his back. Try to save face or be honest? "Pretty much the same thing."

He squeezed her calf where it rested on his waist. "I hear good things about literary agents from Manhattan, too."

"Yeah, we're the last of a dying breed; a true icon of the city," she said. He laughed and it made her smile.

He carried her all the way to the train, a half mile at least, not setting her down until he deposited her in a chair. "Thank you," she said. "I'm fairly certain I couldn't have made it on my own. If you offered this service in Manhattan, you could make a fortune on tips alone."

He sat down beside her. "We could have stopped dancing awhile ago."

"No, we absolutely could not. I loved it." She rested her head on the seat behind her and smiled up at him. "Thanks, Cam, for a great night all around. It's been fun to catch up."

"You think it's over? Girl, it's not over," he said. "You have yet to experience the full Cameron King treatment." He wagged his brows at her, tossing in a wink for good measure.

"I'm not sure what that means, but I suddenly feel the need to guard my virtue," she said, crossing her arms over protectively over her midsection.

He grinned at her and bent down, reaching for her feet. Plucking off her shoes, he tossed them onto the empty seat across from them and began to massage the ball of her foot with his thumb.

"Pretty feet," he commented.

She was thankful her expensive pedicure was still fresh. "Thanks," she muttered dreamily. Whatever he was doing was heaven, a new and unexpected bliss. The train was practically deserted, so she had no qualms about closing her eyes and reveling in the unbidden treatment, going boneless so the only thing holding her upright was the seat behind her. "Did you go to school for this?" she whispered. He advanced from her foot to her ankle and began gently massaging the joint, twisting it in a gentle circle as he rubbed.

"No, but this is what the horses enjoy after a long day on the trail," he said. Her eyes popped open to see if he was kidding, but his intense expression gave nothing away. It was then she realized he was enjoying the experience as much as she was.

"So you're a foot guy," she said, still in the same dreamy, sleepy tone. "That surprises me."

He gave a slight shake of his head. "I'm not a foot guy. I think maybe I'm an Isabelle Landry guy."

"Where are you coming up with this stuff?" she murmured, eyes sliding closed again. He was acting very un-Camlike this evening.

"Don't ruin the moment, Belle," he urged.

And because what he was doing to her foot felt so good, she complied. By the time they arrived at their station he had to rouse her back to wakefulness. When shaking her didn't work, shoving her feet back into her shoes did.

"Ouch." She sat up and glared accusingly at him.

"We're home," he said.

"Oh. That was fast."

"It was an hour. Do you need me to carry you again?"

"No, I can make it. Thanks." In truth, her feet were still killing her, but this was their small town. If anyone saw her riding on Cameron King's back, the gossip mill would have them married by morning. He must have had the same thought because he didn't try to take her hand or place his hand on her back as he had been doing almost instinctively all night.

But when they reached her parents' front porch, he faced her and slid his arms cozily around her middle, his palms warm and firm on her bare back. *Callouses,* she thought. His palms had so many hard earned callouses. Storm had one callous on his middle finger, where his paintbrush often lay.

"Tonight was nice, Belle," he said, tone cozy and intimate.

"It really was," she agreed. She couldn't remember the last time she'd had such a good date, if she ever had. The night had turned cold, and she hadn't worn a coat. Even wrapped in his arms, she was chilly. He noticed and took off his jacket to drape around her, drawing her slightly closer in the process. She tugged his lapels and stood on her toes.

"You look really nice tonight, Cam. Sorry if I didn't tell you that earlier."

He smiled and slipped his hand inside his coat, pressing his palms on her bare back once more. "I think you should wear this dress every day."

She was about to disagree, but then his right hand began smoothing up and down her spine. "I'll think about it," she said.

"Typically, it's customary to end a date with a goodnight kiss," he said. "Even for friends who've known each other as long as we have."

With no thought to Storm, or the town gossips, or anything other than how good it felt to be in his arms, she found herself agreeing. "That's a universal rule, I think."

"I'm glad we agree for once." He dipped his head to hers, but before their lips could meet, the front door was abruptly jerked open.

"Oh, there is someone here," Belle's father said. His stridently cheerful tone felt like a blast of cold water to its hearers. "Martha said she heard people talking. I said it was the wind. Martha, you win," he called over his shoulder before turning back to face them. "Hello, Cameron."

"Hello, Mr. Landry." Cam removed his right hand from Belle's back and held it out for her father to shake.

"I ran into Bill at the mill and he said one of your bulls was sick. I hope it's nothing serious," Mr. Landry said.

"The vet doesn't seem to think so, thank you for your concern," Cam said.

"Um, Dad, we were saying goodnight. I'll be in soon," Belle said because her father was a talker and showed no intention of going back inside.

"Oh. *Oh*," he repeated, realizing for the first time that the two people in front of him were on a date. "Right. Sorry. Carry on." He frowned. "Or don't. Never mind." He backed inside and shut the door.

When Belle turned her face to Cam again, he knew the moment was gone. Her defenses were back up, and they looked more impermeable than ever.

"I really had a nice time tonight," she said formally, easing slightly away from him.

With effort, he suppressed a sigh. Two steps forward, one step back. "It's supposed to be nice tomorrow. Come for a picnic," he said.

She bit her lip and glanced uncertainly at the door.

"You're running out of time," he told her.

She had no idea what that meant from his perspective, but he was right. She had a week left to talk to Layla and convince her to sign a contract. Her eyes gleamed with calculation as she stared at the door. "What time tomorrow?" she asked, infusing her voice with innocence.

"Noon."

She nodded, determined to show up at eleven and have a good, long chat with the elusive Layla. "I'll see you at noon." She tried hard not to emphasize the word "you" and make him suspicious. Cam had a way of seeing through her that was both disconcerting and endearing. She turned to face him again. He leaned down, bypassed her lips, and pressed a soft kiss to her cheek.

"Goodnight, Bucky."

She remained standing on the porch, watching him drive away. Strange how such a hated nickname could sound like a caress when he said it like that.

The next morning, she knew she was in trouble. Before setting out for the King's ranch, she stopped at the store to see her father. No less than six people stopped to congratulate her on her new relationship.

"I always liked them King boys," one of her father's cashiers said.

"They've got a lot of money. A girl who hooks up with them is set for life." This came from the second cashier. Belle turned to the third cashier, waiting.

"They're fine looking and buff, every last one of them. Even the one that's so young he's illegal."

Belle practically ran out of the store, blushing all the way. She threw her bag in the rental car and took off toward the King ranch, her mind stewing with frustration. What was wrong with this backwards little town? Could two people not spend the evening together and keep it private? And for that matter, why did it have to be a big deal? Why did people read forever into one night? She lived in New York. Her absence over the last four years should have made that clear. What would make anyone think one date with Cameron King would be enough to compel her to leave the city she loved, the job she loved, and return to her tiny hometown?

At least she took comfort in the fact that news of her date with Cam wouldn't get back to Storm. Of course she would have to break up with him now that she had realized the imbalance in their relationship. And it wasn't as if they'd ever declared themselves exclusive. She banged her fist on the steering wheel in frustration. One more thing coming home had ruined for her. Before this trip, she had been happy in her lukewarm, no-strings relationship. She had delighted in ordering Storm's life for him.

Then Cameron King intervened by pointing out she was like Storm's mother. Even though he had been speaking in generalities about her personality, he had hit the nail on the head. Storm deserved the opportunity to make decisions for himself. And if he was unwilling to find someone who would allow him to do that, he should find someone who was content to pretend to be his mother because Belle no longer wanted the role.

By the time she reached the halfway point of the King's lane, she had calmed considerably. Breaking up with Storm wouldn't be pleasant, but she felt good about having made the decision. As for the town gossip, what did it matter to her? She didn't live here. Cam was the one who should be upset by it, but he probably wouldn't be. He was strong enough to handle whatever the town threw at him, proven by the fact that he had probably already been the object of gossip ever since his brother married his girlfriend.

She turned off the car and allowed it to coast to a stop in front of the house. Visitors were few and far between on the ranch. Cam would be alerted by the sound of any vehicle, but especially hers, and she didn't want anything to ruin this opportunity to talk to Layla. She could only pray the younger girl would be home and available to have this most important discussion.

Without making a sound, she eased from the car and practically tiptoed up the steps. Letting herself in without knocking was rude, but she couldn't take the chance of alerting anyone to her presence. For that reason she gently pulled the door open, crept inside and toward the kitchen.

Layla sat at the kitchen table, a pad of paper and pen before her. Belle's heart sped with excitement. Most writers preferred to use a computer, but there were still some who preferred to do it the old fashioned way with a pen and paper. Layla apparently fell in the second category.

"Layla."

Belle whispered her name, but Layla still jumped and dropped her pen. "Belle. I didn't hear you come in."

"Sorry about that. I don't want Cam to know I'm here."

"Why? Are you guys fighting?"

"No more than usual. But I came to talk to you."

"To me?" Layla asked, looking surprised. "Why?"

Belle took a breath and plunged in. "It's about your hobby."

Layla looked almost frightened at being found out. "You know about that?"

"I do, and I think it's great. I want to talk to you about taking it a step further."

Layla licked her lips. "This is...unexpected." She would have said more, but the front door banged shut and Belle knew the gig was up.

"Dang it, Belle, I told you noon," Cam said as he strode angrily into the room.

Layla looked uncertainly between them. "Your picnic basket is ready, like you requested, Cam."

"Thank you, Layla," he said. "We'll take it now, please."

Layla turned to the refrigerator, glad for the distraction from the tension now bouncing around the room. She set it on the table beside Cam and backed away until she rested against the counter.

"I'm not ready yet. I want to talk to Layla. Go back outside," Belle commanded.

"No. Layla's busy. She can't talk right now," Cam said. They both turned to look at Layla who now looked like a deer caught in headlights.

"Yes, I can see she's overflowing with work. You can't keep her from talking to me."

"I can," Cam argued. "My ranch, my house, my housekeeper. Let's go."

Sensing she was about to lose in a big way, Belle turned her attention to Layla. "You can talk to me if you want to, Layla. He can't tell you what to do." She grunted when Cam put his shoulder to her stomach and picked her up.

"Could you carry the basket to the car for us, Layla?" Cam interrupted her.

"Uh, right now I'm equally frightened of both of you and unwilling to get in the middle of whatever this is," Layla said.

"Fair enough," Cam said. He held out his arm and she slid the picnic basket onto it. "Thanks," he said.

"You have options," Belle said, still addressing Layla. "You're not a prisoner of this ranch." Cam began striding toward the door with her and the basket. "Take my card," Belle yelled desperately. She dug in her pocket and tossed the card toward Layla but it fluttered listlessly to the ground. "Call me. We'll talk."

The door banged shut, drowning out her last word. Cam knew better than to put her into the passenger side. He put the basket in the passenger side and shoved Belle into the driver's side before crawling in behind her, one hand grasping her pants the whole time to keep her from dashing away.

But he needn't have worried. Belle sat complacently and silently beside him. Knowing her as he did, that was what worried him. He dragged her out of the truck when they reached their destination. He went far enough from the house that it would be a long hike to get back. She stood leaning against the truck while he spread out the blanket and placed the basket on it.

"You coming?" he asked, a challenging glint in his eyes. Would she say no? How angry was she?

She walked sedately toward him and sat gently beside him on the blanket. He remained wary as he handed her the food. It was still early, and she wasn't hungry, but she picked delicately at the bounty. He ate like the ravenous cowboy he was. She sat watching him long after she was finished, until at last he was done.

"That was delicious, thank you," she said sweetly. "And you're right. It's a lovely day for a picnic."

He finally relaxed and managed a smile for her. "You're welcome. And I'm sorry about earlier at the house. I know you don't understand, but I have my reasons for things."

She nodded. "I do understand, and it's okay. Really." She surprised him by resting her palms on his thighs and leaning forward. His heart rate kicked into overdrive as he leaned forward to meet her lips. So intent was he on the impending kiss he almost missed the fact that her finger dipped into his pocket and pulled out his keys.

He lunged for her, but he was too late. She jumped up and sprinted toward the truck. But of course she was wearing uncomfortable shoes, not good for running, and he was able to easily overtake her. He grabbed her around the waist and she started to fight him. For a small, city girl, she was a good fighter, probably because she fought dirty. By the time he finally wrestled her to the blanket and pinned her there, he was panting with exertion and pretty certain he would have some bruises tomorrow.

"You can't keep her from talking to me," she yelled, still trying to squirm away from him.

"Yes I can," he said, furious because he was having such a difficult time holding her in place. She was only one small woman, how could she cause him so much trouble?

"You don't even know what I want to talk to her about," she threw out.

"Yes I do," he said.

"Then tell me," she challenged.

"The story," he said.

She stopped struggling and stared at him in shock. "What?"

"The story in the magazine."

"How…How did you know that?"

"Because a short story gets published in a mainline magazine and a month later you, a successful literary agent, show up out of the blue after you've made no secret of how much you hate it here. It didn't take a genius to put two and two together. I knew as soon as you stepped out of the car."

"But, Cam, she's good. I mean, she's really, really good. I need to talk to her and let her know what's out there for her."

"You can't," he started, then talked over her when she tried to interrupt him. "Layla didn't write it."

That shut her up. "Ivy? She doesn't look like a writer, but it goes to show you never can tell about some people."

"Not Ivy," he said.

Her brows puckered. "Your mom?" She tried and failed to reconcile the beautiful prose with the woman who had so badly deformed the wolf in the painting in Cam's office.

"Not my mom."

There was something significant in his tone. He was trying to tell her something, but what? All of a sudden, she knew. "You wrote it," she whispered.

"I wrote it," he confirmed. His face was newly vulnerable, waiting for her reaction.

She thought of the beautiful story about the husband and wife stranded in the snow. After days of trying to survive, the woman died. Two days later, the husband heard rescuers in the woods, but instead of alerting them to his presence, he laid himself over his wife and chose to die with her instead of live without her. Now that she knew it was him, she could see him in the story, his strength and loyalty. What surprised her so much was the romance. Never in a million years would she have guessed a man wrote the sweet and sensitive piece.

"Say something," he urged.

But she couldn't. She had no words. Pinned as she was, movement was difficult, but she could still raise her head. So she did. She lifted her lips to his and brushed them with a soft kiss.

With something that sounded like a groan, he let go of her hands where he had them pinned over her head. Drawing her as close as possible, he kissed her. When he couldn't get her as close as he wanted, he twisted them so they were lying on their sides, cinching her tight against his chest. Her fingers stabbed into his hair and drew him closer, too.

Part of her understood she was kissing Cameron King, the guy she had known almost all her life, the person who had driven her crazy for all of that time. The other part of her reminded her this was the man who had written the story that had made her cry, the story that had been so riveting she flew thousands of miles to meet with him. And she couldn't decide which fact was more compelling. Then she shut off her brain and allowed herself simply to feel, to delight in his kiss. There had never been a kiss like this one, at least not for her. Like everything Cam did, he was thorough and perfect. After a while she began to feel boneless, and then senseless, and then as if she were skittering out of control.

Thankfully, he was the one who broke off, pushing her away from him and collapsing back onto the blanket. He didn't let her go completely, however. One hand remained at the base of her skull, drawing her down onto his chest.

They lay in silence a few minutes, trying to recover enough to talk. Unsurprisingly, she was the first one to find her voice.

"You have to let me represent you," she said.

He didn't let her go when he said, "Over my dead body."

CHAPTER 13

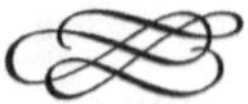

She propped her elbows on his chest and looked down at him. "Why not?"

"Why do you think?" he asked. "It would ruin my reputation as a rancher in this town. No one would ever take me seriously again."

With difficulty, she refrained from telling him how stupid it was to let others' opinions rule his life. After all, hadn't she told her boss she had to come here and convince the author for this very reason? These were her people; she knew how they thought. And he was correct. He would be an outcast. No one would ever take him seriously as a rancher again. He would find acclaim as a writer, only to lose face as a rancher. And the ranch was in his blood, he had said so.

She scooted up so she could press her palms to his cheeks. "I can keep your identity safe. No one has to know. We'll stick with a pseudonym. Lots of authors, even famous authors, remain anonymous. You can trust me to keep the secret, Cam. You know you can."

He looked up at her, so passionate and intense, and knew then that he loved her. Maybe it had happened gradually over the last few days, or maybe it had happened the second she stepped out of her rental car. She was all wrong for him, at least on paper. Yet somehow she was perfect. He couldn't railroad her, and she made him laugh; two things no other woman had ever accomplished. But, much as he loved her, he couldn't do what she wanted.

He put his hand up to cup her cheek. "I can't do it, Belle."

"Do you have any idea how much money we're talking about?"

"I don't need money," he said. The ranch was doing fine without any income writing would bring in.

"But I do. Do you have any idea how much is at stake? I put my career on the line for this."

"You shouldn't have," he said simply. "You know how it is here."

"Cam, you have to do this. Please, I am begging you, and you know I never beg."

To his horror, he saw tears sparkling in her eyes. His gut twisted with pain and he wanted to do whatever possible to make those tears go away, even if it meant giving in. "Tell me why it's so important to you, and don't say it's your job. We both know better." She was good at her job, and she was persuasive. Even if she didn't sign him, she would no doubt return to where she had been which was the top of the heap.

She took a deep, shaky breath and let it out slowly. "Growing up, I had no friends. Oh, I had Coy," she said before she could interrupt. "And you tolerated me grudgingly, but it wasn't like having real friends. You guys had each other and your teammates. You didn't need or want me; I was along for the ride. But I had books, lots and lots of books. I found friends there. I traveled to interesting places. In a way, the characters I read about in books became real to me. They made me who I am and kept me from being so horribly alone. I wanted to be able to do for others what books did for me. But I'm a horrible writer. No, really. I'm honest enough to admit it. I tried. I failed. When I realized I didn't have the talent, I devoted my life to promoting other people who did. You think I'm good at what I do, Cam, but you're wrong. I'm excellent, and I know how good you are. You could be the next Hemingway of our generation."

"I don't like Hemingway," he said.

"Then insert your favorite author and picture yourself doing better than him," she said.

"My favorite author is a woman," he said.

She pressed her hands to her temples. "My brain is going to explode if you tell me one more shocking fact about yourself. But you get the point. If you don't publish your work, you are denying the world something they need. And you're denying yourself the opportunity to try something new."

For once, she remained silent while she allowed him to think. Whereas with anyone else she would be able to browbeat them into getting her way, that would never work with Cam. He was as strong as she was and no amount of arguing would win him over. She could only hope that after having made her case, he would somehow see things her way.

He lifted his hand and wound it in her hair, his thumb stroking her jawbone. "You're here for another week, right?"

"Not if I get an answer today," she said hopefully.

He smiled. "How about we make a deal?"

She gripped his shirt tightly in her fists. "What sort of deal?"

"I will agree to be published if you agree to spend the next entire week here at the ranch and do everything I ask of you."

"Why do I feel like there's a catch in there somewhere?" she asked.

"Next Friday is Founder's Day."

She sat up and tried to scramble away from him, but only succeeded in falling on her backside. "No, Cam, you can't be serious."

"I am," he said placidly.

"You can't make me do that," she said. Founder's Day was the town's equivalent of July 4th. Every year the entire community came together for a day of corny games, food, fireworks, and a dance. And every year without fail, something had gone horribly wrong for Belle. How could she not have taken Founder's Day into account when she arranged this trip? If she had, she would have changed her reservation to Siberia to ensure she was as far away as possible.

"You're right. I can't make you do it," Cam said reasonably. "But then neither will I agree to be published."

She blew out a breath. It was a sign of how much she hated Founder's Day that she was wavering.

"Come on," Cam cajoled. "I'll let you read my book."

She sat bolt upright, her heart rate accelerating to stroke level. "You wrote a book?" When she went searching for the author of the story, she figured she would have to coax her/him into writing a book. To learn one had already been written was akin to finding a copy of the Declaration of Independence in a garage sale purchase.

"I wrote a book," he said.

"What's it about? What's the word count? Is it finished? Is it good? Can I have it now?" She tried to stand, but he grasped her waist and pulled her back down beside him, putting his arm around her and drawing her close. She rested her head on his shoulder and looked up at him with wide, excited eyes.

"You haven't answered my proposal."

She bit her lip. "What am I supposed to tell my parents? Do you know what people are going to say when I move in here for a week? They already think we're dating."

"We are dating," he said, startling her with his matter-of-fact tone. "As for your parents, tell them you're working, which will be true. You already said the work setup here was better. It's ridiculous for you to keep driving two hours a day when there's so much work to be done on my book."

"But I'll hurt their feelings if I leave them," she said.

He was surprised she meant it, and he was learning she wasn't as tough as she let on. "We'll visit them in town and we can have them out for dinner one night."

She closed her eyes and burrowed her head in his shoulder, secretly pleased at how he already spoke of them as a unit. Later, there would be time to figure out the tricky fact that they lived thousands of miles apart and wanted two different things from life. For now, it was enough to know he was the one she had been looking for. The author she had been looking for, she hastily amended herself. And he wanted her here. For everything else, they would take it a day at a time.

<h1 style="text-align:center">CHAPTER 14</h1>

Cam would have remained all day, reveling in the afterglow of their first kiss and tentative step toward establishing a relationship. But of course Belle had other ideas. She was anxious to get back to the house and begin reading his book, and he had to admit that was almost as gratifying as kissing her had been.

He hadn't shared his work with anyone, hadn't told a soul he liked to write. He had submitted the story to the magazine on a whim after a long, hard, lonely day, and hadn't had any feedback other than the fact that they published him. Hearing Belle, of all people, tell him he had talent and ability was like winning a Pulitzer, only more so because he was personally vested in her opinion. And he loved writing. Putting down on paper all he felt but wasn't able to express out loud alleviated his pent up emotions, allowing them a safe outlet. At least it had been safe until Belle found him. But he did trust her to keep his secret.

"Cam, please let's go. I'm dying here." She tugged his lapels, trying unsuccessfully to pull him up, and then she froze, staring at him with a considering expression. "Do you think there are ticks out here? Do you need me to search you?" Her hands traced the contours of his chest and lingered.

"No, I think we're safe from ticks here. You know, you're sort of obsessed with ticks."

"I suppose," she said, blushing faintly. "I've been thinking about them an inordinate amount lately. Now can we go?"

"Yes." He stood to gather the blanket and basket, but by the time he was fully upright she was finished with the task. She threw the items into the truck and hopped in, not waiting for his help. To torment her, he drove slowly back to the house. She knew and clucked her tongue impatiently a few times before reaching her foot over in an attempt to press the gas pedal.

"Don't even think about it." He caught her leg, but instead of tossing it back onto her side, he held onto it, pressing his palm to the inside of her knee.

"This isn't comfortable," she complained.

"Then move closer," he said, and she did, sliding close and slipping her arms around his waist when he put his arm around her shoulders.

"There's something to be said for a large truck and no seatbelts," she said.

"Score one for Montana," he said.

She frowned, not liking that he was keeping a tally. This wouldn't end with anything less than her return to New York, and if he didn't know that then he was more of a romantic than she realized. But rather than ruin the moment she remained mute, once again pillowing her head against his shoulder. He was so *solid*. Not only in body mass, but in spirit, as well. He was utterly unshakable, which could be sort of annoying when she thought about it. How could she ever hope to win against him? She was used to winning all the time.

"What's the frown for?" he asked.

"I was thinking you're never going to let me win," she said.

"You've got that right."

"But I don't want to lose all the time. That's no fun. I have no leverage with you."

That wasn't true, but he didn't tell her. The sight of her tears had miraculously made him want to give her whatever she wanted in order to make her stop crying. Seeing her in pain or upset would have the same effect, he was certain. No need to tell her that, though.

"We'll figure it out," he said easily. "Maybe we'll both eventually want the same thing and won't have to fight all the time." Working together for a common goal with Belle was enough to send his heart spinning. Right now he was attracted to her and in love with her, but he held no illusions about the difficulties that lay before them. Despite having grown up together, they were from two different worlds. He only had this week to try and convince her they could find compromise before he might lose her forever.

She smiled. "If we were ever on the same team, we could achieve world domination."

"That's the plan," he said. They pulled up to the house and he put the truck in park.

"Let's go get your book," she said excitedly. She reached for the door, but he held her back.

"First things first: we have to go into town and get your things."

Her face took on a pouty expression and she crossed her arms over her chest. "Cam, you're teasing me."

Because he had never seen her pout before, he was fascinated by her reaction. "You really want to read my book, don't you?" he asked, awed.

"More than anything I've ever wanted before," she said seriously. "Anything."

He reached for her, sliding her across the seat and into his arms. "More than anything, Isabelle?" Bending down, he pressed his lips to her neck, biting softly.

"Well, almost anything," she said, her voice not quite steady. He raised his face to meet hers, but a loud tap on his window interrupted them.

"You're blocking your poor, handicapped brother's ramp with this truck," Coy announced, trying and failing to stifle his grin.

Cam turned around, scanning the horizon. "Where is he?"

"He's in the barn. But eventually he'll come out, and he'll want to use it." He grinned wickedly at his brother before ducking his head to peer inside the truck. "What do we have here? Hey, it's Belle."

"Hey, Coy," she said, trying to suppress a laugh. She had always found Coy entertaining.

Cam broke their eye line by inserting himself between them. "Fine. We'll move. Tell Layla I won't be home for supper tonight. I'm going to get Belle's things. She's moving in with me." With that, he rolled up the window and drove away, leaving Coy gaping after them in shock.

Belle laughed. "You're naughty, leaving his head ready to explode like that."

"It's about time he had a taste of his own medicine. I've been on the receiving end of his pranks for too many years."

"Why did you never pay him back before now?" she asked.

"Because I didn't have much to be amused about before now, or anyone to make me smile," he said.

"Aw, Cam, you're really good at the mushy stuff."

He glanced at her, eyes kindling with serious intent. "Not with anyone else, Belle. Buckle your seatbelt; we're almost to the road."

She reached for her seatbelt, thought better of it and scooted over, buckling herself in the middle seat beside him. "I do love these Montana trucks."

* * *

An hour later, they arrived at Belle's parents' house in town.

"This is not going to go well," Belle said.

"This will be fine," Cam assured her.

"Since when are you an optimist?" she asked.

"Since you came back to town," he said.

"Cam," she exclaimed, pressing her hands over her ears.

"Is the sweetness freaking you out?" he guessed.

"Completely, but also I...I like it." She leaned over the seat and kissed his cheek.

That was good because he had no plans to stop. Once tapped, the well of his unspent affection ran deep, and he found he wanted to lavish all of it on Belle, who had also missed out on her fair share of softness in life.

"Let's get this done," he said.

She led him to the house and opened the door. "Mom, I'm home." There was no answer, and she grimaced. "She must be at the store. I really didn't want to have to do this there. Let's pack and go."

He sat on her bed, watching her cool efficiency as she packed. In less time than he would have thought possible, the task was finished. He carried her bags to the truck, stuffed them in the bed, and they drove to her father's store.

Belle felt like every eye was on them as they made the unending procession to her father's office. Since there were only six people in the store, she was correct. All activity came to a halt and focused on her and Cam, who made matters worse by draping his arm possessively around her shoulders, as if they were in high school instead of two adult professionals. Amazingly, she found she minded less than she should, especially given her status as an independent woman. If she were being honest, she enjoyed the buffering security of his embrace. She would need it as she attempted to explain what she was about to do to her parents. More than that, though, she enjoyed showing the town that she—awkwardly geeky Isabelle Landry—was on the arm of the great and mighty Cameron King. Would she ever not be that awkward little girl? Cam spoke, jarring her from her thoughts.

"Ready?" he asked when they reached the door.

"As I'll ever be," she answered.

"Don't tell me Bucky Landry is afraid," he whispered. She remembered he had said those same words to her once when she came up to bat in gym class. Being more than a little clumsy, she had been terrified of the ball.

Don't tell me Bucky Landry is afraid, Cam had taunted from the pitcher's mound, because of course a King was pitching. If there was an athletic feat to be performed, one of them would lead the charge.

She answered now as she had then. "I ain't afraid of nothin'," Then she turned the handle and stepped inside her father's office.

CHAPTER 15

Thanks to Cam, the conversation with her parents went better than she could have hoped. First of all, they treated him like royalty when he entered the office. In their neck of the woods, he practically was. The Kings were some of the area's first white settlers, had practically founded the ensuing town. Since then their wealth and status had only grown. And he had proximity in his favor. Belle had the suspicion her mother thought if Belle and Cam became involved, Belle would either move home or return to visit more often. She must have passed along her theory to Belle's father because they both acted like Cam was their long lost son, patting his shoulder possessively and chattering enthusiastically about neighbors and cows.

Belle was impatient to get it over with, but Cam took her hand and gave it a squeeze, reminding her to be patient. When the long conversation finally came to an end, she opened her mouth to speak, but Cam preempted her.

"Mr. and Mrs. Landry, I hate to ask, since you only got Belle back, but I was wondering if you would mind if she stayed at the ranch for the second part of her vacation. She's helping me with a project, and I need her."

They blinked at him before turning to look worriedly at Belle.

"At your ranch with all you boys?" her mother squeaked. Belle could practically hear her mind click with all the ensuing gossip such an endeavor would cause.

"And my sister-in-law and our housekeeper, don't forget. Belle would share a room with her. We're starting to even out on the female to male ratio now." He bestowed on them his most charming, parent-wooing smile and it seemed to be working.

She watched her parents visibly relax. "Well, if you need her," her father said warily.

"I really do," Cam said, clutching Belle's hand to his chest. "Plus I want her there, to be honest. We're getting to know each other again, and I would really like the chance to spend some time with her before she heads back to New York. I know it's selfish of me, but I hope you'll understand."

"Oh, well, then," her father mumbled, flustered. "I guess that would be okay. Martha? That okay with you?" He glanced over his shoulder at his wife.

"Okay by me." Her mother beamed, glancing furtively between Cam and Belle, mind whirring with flower arrangements and wedding colors. Of course they'd have to get someone from Billings to cater. A King wedding would expect nothing less than the best.

"I'll call you," Belle added hastily, miming a phone with her pinky and thumb, as if her parents didn't know what one looked like. Her parents regarded her as if she'd flipped her lid before returning their combined and adoring gaze back to Cam. Ten minutes into her new relationship and he was already their bygone favorite.

"And we'll make sure and have you out to dinner one night this week. Have you ever been to the ranch?" Cam continued, putting the final nails in the coffin of her parents' abject and enduring devotion.

"Not since you boys were little," her mother answered, puffing importantly. An invitation to the ranch. Wait until the ladies at church heard about this.

"It's a beautiful spread," her father added. His tone was informational, as if Cam might not know.

"Thank you, I believe so, too. We already retrieved Belle's things, so we'll let you get back to your work here." He tugged Belle toward the door, but she broke free and hugged both her parents, kissing their cheeks.

"I feel like I'm abandoning them," she said when she exited the office. After a four-year absence, she hadn't realized how much she missed them.

Cam paused. "You don't have to do this if you don't want. I don't want you to have any regrets about leaving them."

She let out a slow breath. "It's okay. I'm feeling maudlin, I guess. It will go away as soon as I see your book. Now can we *please* go home?"

He checked his watch. "By the time we get back, we will have missed supper. Let's pick up a pizza." Noting her mutinous expression, he hastened to continue. "It will only take a few minutes. Please. I'm hungry, and you know how I get when I'm hungry."

"Okay. But I'm beginning to get the feeling you're leading me on a merry chase."

"Trust me," he said. They ordered their pizza at the local shop attached to one side of her father's store and waited in silence until it was ready, fielding curious glances from everyone who entered the small shop. Cam grabbed the pizza, along with a couple of sodas, and carried them to his truck. He handed the pizza to her so he could drive, and she realized how hungry she was as soon as the smell hit her.

"This is going to be cold by the time we get home."

It thrilled him more than a little how easily she referred to his ranch as home. "We're not going home," he said.

"Cam, you said," she began, but he interrupted her.

"I said to trust me, and I stand by that request." He drove to a park at the edge of town and parked under a streetlight, one of only four in the entire town. Reaching over the seat behind him, he pulled out the blanket from their picnic, along with a black briefcase. He tapped it. "My book is in here. I was carrying it from the office to the house when I saw your car in the drive, so I tossed it in the truck on my way in the house."

"Gimme," she demanded, extending her arms to him, an eager and urgent light in her eyes. She sounded desperate, half crazed with frenzied excitement.

"You said you were hungry."

"I'll eat later. *Please.*" She clasped her hands together, literally begging.

"Belle, eat first and then read. It will only take a few minutes. I want you in the best frame of mind possible when you read it. Please." His hand reached out and stroked the side of her head. She leaned into his touch, releasing a pent up sigh.

"Okay."

"Just like that you're agreeing with me?"

"I must be weakened by hunger." She opened the sodas while he arranged the box of pizza between them. She ate in record time, so quickly she was sure she would have heartburn soon.

"Done," she declared, tossing back her soda and setting the can down with a triumphant thump. After carefully cleaning her hands, she reached for the briefcase and opened it, reverently pulling out the bound stack of papers. She flipped to the end, searching for the page number. "That's the perfect length for a first novel." She smoothed her hand over the book and turned to look at him. "Now. I want you to read it to me."

He choked on a sip of soda. "Me? Why?"

"Because you're the author. You'll read it the way I'm supposed to hear it."

"Is this what you do with all your authors?" he asked. It seemed oddly intimate to him, but maybe this was how her process worked.

"Of course not. But this is special, you're special, and I want to hear it coming from you. I'll give it a more critical review later. Right now I want you to read to me so I can have the unmitigated pleasure of hearing it in your voice."

"I don't know, Belle," he said, sounding uncharacteristically shy.

She pressed her palm to his chest and leaned closer. "Please, Cam. *Please.* It would mean a lot for me to hear it coming from you. It would mean the world."

"All right," he agreed quietly. She set aside their trash and reached for the blanket, settling it around them to keep off the encroaching chill. He did her one better by shifting to her side of the truck to avoid the steering wheel, and then pulling her into his arms. They nestled a little to get comfortable, and then he started to read. His voice was low and sonorous by her ear. She closed her eyes and immediately lost herself in the lyrical prose. He was a descriptive writer, and she had no trouble imagining his books on the bestseller list. But all thoughts of her job fled as she lost herself in the book. One of her hands curled into the buttons of his shirt, and she was transported to a world he'd created, lost in his beautiful words, meeting new friends for the first time, friends he'd written as if specifically for her. For Belle, who loved books more than anything else in the world, it was a special kind of magic, more so because it came from him, this boy turned man who was beginning to mean so much to her in so many different ways.

The story was deep literary fiction about a young man who, beaten up and downtrodden by circumstances, ended up murdering a police officer. Overcome by his actions, he fled and decided to change his life. For the next twenty years, he attempted to make amends by using his life to make a difference, giving himself tirelessly to others and never revealing his secret past. Meanwhile, the cop's younger sister devoted those same twenty years to tracking down her brother's killer, eventually realizing the man she had secretly been in love with for the past three years was the same man she had been searching for. The characters were perfectly written. Cam spared them no pity. Instead of making them flawless, he showed how their insurmountable flaws had shaped their lives. The hero's need for atonement neatly paralleled the heroine's need for vengeance, intertwining their lives throughout the book.

At her urging, he read the entire book. It was one in the morning when he finally finished, and Belle was crying. Not watery eyes and a few sniffles, but wracking sobs and rivers of tears. The book hadn't ended happily, at least not in the classic sense. There had been atonement and redemption, but no happy ending for the two star-crossed lovers. She loved it because he remained true to his characters and true to their stories, but she hated it because she had become vested in their lives and one of them died.

Cam remained silent, taking her tears as a hopeful sign she had liked the book. But her first words caught him by surprise.

"I am so good," she said, wiping her eyes. "I am so, incredibly good. I *knew* the person who wrote that story was going to be worth whatever it took to get a contract, and I was right. It's gratifying to be so good at what I do." She reached for a tissue and wiped her nose. "As for you," she turned toward him and set the book back in the briefcase, freeing his hands. "I think you are cruel for not allowing your characters to ride off into the sunset together."

He smiled, immensely relieved she liked his work enough to become so involved in the story. "You need a happy ending, huh?"

She nodded. "The happiest."

"Let see what I can do to help," he said, and then he kissed her.

By the time they arrived back at the ranch, it was three in the morning. Instead of risking waking Layla by sneaking into her room, they decided Belle should sleep on the couch that night. Cam would have given her his bed and taken the couch, but even among his family and employees there was gossip. Neither of them wanted to start rumors about Belle sleeping in his bed.

The next morning, she was still fast asleep when he woke. He perched on the edge of the couch and gently brushed the hair off her face, smiling when she blinked sleepily at him.

"What time is it?" she croaked.

"Six."

"In the morning?"

"Yes. I overslept, thanks to you."

"Do I have to get up now?"

"No. I thought you might be more comfortable sleeping in a bed. You can use mine; I'm going to work."

"'Kay," she said, closing her eyes. She would have fallen back asleep if he left her alone.

"Want me to carry you?" he offered.

She sat up, blinking sleepily. "I can make it. Where is it?"

"Last door on the right," he said.

"'Kay," she repeated. He helped untangle her from the covers and offered his hand to pull her up, kissing her tenderly while she was still sleep-warm and groggy. She stumbled down the hall and paused at his door to give him a sleepy smile and wave.

Something inside him clenched at the sight of her sleep-mussed hair and tousled appearance heading into his room. *More.* He was determined to do whatever necessary to make their temporary arrangement permanent in order to have a lifetime of mornings together, and he only had a week to figure out how to make it happen.

He refused to consider the possibility that he might fail. He had never failed at anything he determined to do, and he had never been more determined than he was to make Isabelle Landry his forever.

CHAPTER 16

$\mathcal{B}$elle woke in strange surroundings with no sense of alarm. Despite her disorientation, there was something recognizable. Then she took a breath, inhaling Cam's familiar scent and remembered. She was in his room, in his bed. Snuggling down into the covers with a smile of delight, she closed her eyes and inhaled again. She could stay here all day, reveling in the comfort and warmth. There hadn't been one time in the last four years she had indulged in sleeping in, and today was no exception. No matter what time it was, she knew Cam had already been up and waiting on her for hours.

She propped herself on her elbows and scanned the room. The bed was large, probably king size. *No pun intended.* The comforter was white and downy, the sheets and pillowcases were white, too, creating a pristine environment. There was another painting of a wolf on the opposite wall; this one only had three legs and a tail twice the size of his body. Belle guffawed before covering her mouth with the blanket. Next time she saw Mrs. King, she would be hard-pressed not to die laughing from the memory of the woman's horrid painting skills.

The house felt empty as Belle crept to the living room for her things. She gathered them and returned to Cam's bedroom, realizing as she did so the room was massive. She wondered if it had been his

"

parents' suite when they lived there. Somehow it seemed appropriate Cam, the new head of the family, would take over his parents' room. She showered in his bathroom, enjoying the extravagant size of everything. She loved her apartment in Manhattan, but it was tiny, the shower barely big enough to enfold her. In fact Cam's shower was bigger than her entire bathroom. *Score one for Montana,* she thought and then hastily pushed the thought away. *No tallies.*

When she emerged with her hair styled and makeup applied, she felt ready to start the day. A quick glance at the clock told her it was nine thirty. Still early by some standards, but practically the middle of the day on a ranch.

Layla was in the kitchen when Belle entered.

"Good morning," Layla said cheerfully.

"Good morning," Belle returned, feeling uncharacteristically self-conscious. What did the family think of this arrangement? Without revealing Cam's book as the buffer that brought her here, did they think she was moving in of her own volition? How did that make her appear in their eyes?

"Thank you for taking me in like this, Layla," she said, helping herself to a cup of coffee from the nearly full pot. She wondered if Layla kept coffee on for the men all day long. She wanted to offer an explanation or justification for her presence, but she couldn't without breaking Cam's confidence.

"We're thrilled," Layla said, sounding sincere.

"Why?" Belle asked curiously. "It seems like I would be more trouble than I'm worth. Extra mess and an extra mouth to feed, and I assume Cam asked if I could share your room. Plus, let's be honest, I'm not the most tactful person to have around."

"We like you fine," Layla said with a sweet smile. "And even if we didn't, we would put up with you for Cam's sake because of how you've changed him."

"Me? I haven't changed him." The kissing and sweet words were new, but otherwise he was the same Cam he had always been—funny, competitive, solid, occasionally aggravating and stubborn.

"He smiles now. Not only smiles, but laughs. Do you know in all the years I've lived here I have never once heard Cam laugh out loud? He's always been Mr. Serious and In Charge, all business, all the time, totally uncomfortable with any emotion. Then you show up and on your first night here he's laughing like a kid and disappearing to leap into the spring. You're good for him."

Belle blinked at her, dumbfounded. With her formidable personality, she knew she was a lot for a man to handle. She had always viewed herself as more of a liability than an asset. Any man who wanted to be with her would have to put up with a lot. But now someone in Cam's family was telling her she was good for him, that she made him better, younger, happier. And, as astonishing as that information was, she realized the same could be said for him. *He* was good for *her*. He made her laugh. He made her take life and herself less seriously. He caused her to think about something other than success at all costs. It was an anomaly that two such driven, career minded people brought out each other's lighter sides, but who else could? Either of them alone would crush mere mortals.

Layla looked like she wanted to say more, but at that moment Cam appeared in the doorway. He came to stand behind Belle's chair before leaning over to kiss the top of her head, an affectionate little peck that made her heart squeeze with a sweetness that was almost painful in its rightness.

"Did you just get up?"

"No," she lied. "I've been up for hours, and you know how I like to keep busy. So I weather-stripped your windows and re-grouted the tile in your bathroom. I was going to fix some loose shingles on the roof, but I'm feeling lazy. I might let that go for today."

"Sounds like you've been busy. I hope you're not too tired to spend the rest of the day with me."

"I'm refueling with coffee," she told him, holding her cup aloft. "Do you have time for a cup?"

"Sure," he said. He took a step toward the coffeepot, but Layla anticipated him and had a cup ready and waiting. She handed it to him with a smile and made herself scarce by disappearing from the room.

"She's sweet," Belle said.

"Yes she is."

"You were never tempted to date her yourself?"

He smiled at the hint of jealousy in her tone as he sank down beside her. "I think all of us were tempted when she first showed up. She was the first girl here since our mother. She arrived all scared, proud, and pretty—more in need of care and protection than she even realized. But from the first moment they eyed each other, Cade laid claim to her and she to him. They're suited to each other. She and I aren't, although I love her like a sister. It's fun to have a sister, especially one who cooks."

She closed the distance between them and pressed a kiss to his lips.

"Not that I'm complaining, but what was that for?"

"Because I like you," she said matter-of-factly.

"If we're using kisses to express our feelings now, I heartily approve of that plan. But you're going to have to set that coffee aside and come here if you want me to reciprocate properly."

"While that's a tempting offer, I would prefer not to canoodle in your kitchen while your brother's girlfriend is dusting in the next room. Call me old-fashioned." She sipped her coffee. "What's on the agenda for today, Mr. King?"

"It's like I said before. I want you to spend the day with me, getting acclimated to the ranch."

"You make it sound like the ranch is a mystical foreign land. I'm from here, you know."

"With all due respect to your parents, you've always lived in town. That's vastly different than life on a ranch. While you've lived in Montana, you haven't had the full Montana experience. That changes starting today."

"Are you trying to make me fall in love with Montana?" she asked.

"Not just Montana," he said. By the time the week was over, he wanted her to love him, his ranch, his family, and their town. He wanted her to understand roots, family, and community. It was a tall order, but he was pretty sure he could swing it with a little help from his friends.

"And when do we work on our super-secret project?" she asked, tossing him an exaggerated wink that made him chuckle.

"When there's time, super sleuth," he said.

"Okay, but it needs to be ready to the point where I can present it to my boss when I return in a few days. And I need to prepare a contract for you. You should have a lawyer look over it before you sign."

"Why? Do you plan on cheating me?"

"No, it will be a standard contract. But I recommend the same thing to all my clients."

"Thank you, but I've read enough contracts in my time to understand the fine print. I think I'll skip the lawyer."

"Suit yourself, but don't complain when I secretly make my commission forty percent," she said.

"Let's make it fifty fifty and share everything equally," he said, and tossed the exaggerated wink back to her.

"Hoo, boy," she murmured, cheeks heating with a flush that made him laugh again. She finished the last of her coffee and stood to rinse her mug. He threw back the rest of his coffee, rinsed his mug, and they walked outside.

"We're heading to the barn," she announced.

"See, it's those powers of perception that made you valedictorian," he said.

"But there are horses in the barn. You may have forgotten, but horses and I don't do so well together."

"Oh, I haven't forgotten. But that was then. This is now," he said.

"I'm not sure what your impression of Manhattan is, but there is nothing there that, in the last four years, would have miraculously turned me into a horse person."

"I understand that. But last time you were here, you tried to ride by yourself. Today you ride with me." He brought out his big, black stallion—the one he used when he wanted to ride for pleasure and not for ranch work. The horse pranced excitedly, knowing he was going to get the chance to run in a little while, then stood patiently while Cam quickly saddled him while Belle watched, wary and nervous.

He picked Belle up, set her on the horse, and swung up into the saddle behind her.

"Are we working today?" she asked, aiming for a professional tone to cover her fear as the horse began to move. "Are there more cows to deliver?"

"There are always more cows to deliver, and there is always work to be done. But not for us, not today. Today we're riding for pleasure. I'm going to show you what I like to do for fun." His hand rested on her waist, thumb smoothing gently over her hip bone. Whether it was his intent to soothe her or he had nothing else to do with his hand, she had no idea. Either way she relaxed and leaned into him, settling against his solid and enveloping warmth. Of course she knew better than to judge a man by his body, a lofty precept harder to remember when she was this close to his chiseled chest and abs.

He led the horse away from the house and barn at a walk, but as soon as they reached the open pastures, he urged him into a run. Belle tried not to scream, but she was petrified. She had no idea it was possible to go so fast on a horse. Everything was a dizzying blur. Her hands covered her eyes. Beneath them, she squeezed her lids tightly shut, unwilling to see the world spinning by at such a furious pace.

Cam peeled her hands away and held them in her lap. "Open your eyes," he commanded.

"No way," she squeaked.

"Are you chicken?"

She had never been more chicken in her life, but there was still that part of her that couldn't stand to lose face in front of Cameron King. Slowly, she pried her eyes open. Swallowing down her panic, she forced herself to take a deep breath, and then another.

The wind in her face felt good, cooling her overheated cheeks. Short as it was, her hair whipped around her head until she was sure she would probably never get it untangled, but she suddenly didn't care. Lighthearted for the first time in what felt like forever, she laughed. The wind caught the sound and blew it away.

Beneath her, the horse seemed to be laughing, too. It wasn't so much the puffing sound he made as his breath blew out, but the joyful way he held his body, stretching his legs as if trying to eat up as much ground as possible. For the first time, she began to understand the symbiotic relationship between horse and rancher. Ranchers needed horses to help on the ranch, and horses needed a purpose. This horse's purpose was to run, and run he did.

She began to relax her grip, melting into Cam behind her. Instead of locking her knees on the horse and gripping the pommel, she rested her back against Cam and flung her arms open wide. Closing her eyes, she allowed herself to feel the wind sifting her body while the horse's rhythmic pounding made her feel a connection to nature she had never felt before. *This* was why people had owned horses for thousands of years. This was why they were considered majestic animals and pets of kings. Because, not only were they useful, but they were *fun*. Allowing the horse to run full tilt was like riding the best roller coaster of her life, especially because Cam sat behind her, keeping her safe.

Eventually he reined the horse in to a walk. She wondered why, but was too breathless to complain. Maybe it was because the horse needed a break, although it appeared undaunted. In fact, it almost seemed to resent the fact that Cam had slowed it to a walk. *Something we have in common,* she thought. Now that she realized how much she loved it, she wanted to run for much longer. But Cam never did anything without cause, and she was certain now was no exception.

She began to understand his reasoning when they reached the end of the field. Ahead lay a dense forest. The horse probably would have injured itself if it had run full-blast into the crowded growth. They entered at a careful walk. The trees were so close together and dense it suddenly felt like night. The darkness was accompanied by a reverential hush. Belle shuddered at the sudden change in temperature and atmosphere. Her anxiety began to rear its ugly head again but Cam, anticipating her, leaned down to whisper in her ear.

"Don't go faint-hearted on me now. Hang on a little longer. We're almost there."

There? Where was there? She thought he was taking her for a run, to show her what his horse could do, but that must have been the warm up to his true plan. After about a half hour of walking slowly through the trees, the forest emptied out onto another meadow. This one was dotted with purple, pink and yellow wildflowers. It was a breathtaking, beautiful sight.

"I can see why you brought me here," she said. "It's beautiful."

"It is beautiful," he agreed. "But this isn't the end. Be patient."

"My middle name is patience," she said.

He laughed. "What is it, really?"

"Persephone," she said miserably. She had never liked her middle name.

"That's pretty," he said.

"What's yours?"

"Mitchell," he said.

"I like that," she said.

"We'll have to start a list of names we like," he said. His arm tightened on her waist, drawing her back against him. He brushed her hair aside and pressed his lips to her neck. "You never know when you might need a list of names."

She had no reply to that statement. Part of her was elated at what he was hinting, and part of her was petrified. More and more, she was becoming afraid of how quickly things were progressing and, worse, how they would end. And an ending seemed inevitable. Neither would be good at a long distance relationship. From her perspective, it was all or nothing. But all for him was Montana and Manhattan for her was nonnegotiable.

Thankfully Cam didn't seem to expect a reply from her. Instead of putting any expectations on her, he seemed to be letting her glimpse his heart. Knowing how closely he guarded it, she took it for the gift it was. They rode in comfortable silence a few more minutes, and then he pointed to a spot in the distance. "There."

Before them was a waterfall. Thanks to the rocky terrain of the area, there were several waterfalls, so it wasn't as if she had never seen one before. But this one must be special for him to bring her all this way to see it. And when they came close enough for her to see details, she realized why it was special.

He put his finger to his lips, vaulted from the saddle and reached up to lift her down. He also opened his saddlebag and pulled out a high-powered rifle. He pointed to a flat spot between two boulders. The area was littered with pine needles and she wondered if it was he who had placed the pine there as a cushion. They sat. He leaned the rifle against a boulder and put his arm around her. She rested her head on his chest and watched the action at the stream.

Less than a hundred yards in front of them, salmon jumped out of the water, trying desperately to make their way upstream. Most of them didn't make it, and not because the stream was steep. A large grizzly bear stood in the water, picking off the fish like flies at a picnic. Each swat of his huge paw netted a fish. He quickly bit off the head, discarded the body, and reached for another fish, greedy with his lack of ambition.

Realistically Belle knew she should feel afraid. They were only a football field from the most dangerous mammal in the country, but with Cam beside her, she didn't feel afraid. The bear was overfed and feeling lazy. So lazy he didn't bother to pause between fish to clean his bloody muzzle. He simply kept eating, happily devouring his meal before tossing it away. As long as they kept their distance and remained quiet, the bear would leave them alone. And if not, Cam had his gun. At the very least, he would scare it away.

Having decided all this in her mind, she relaxed and enjoyed the show. Despite growing up here, she had never seen a salmon or a grizzly in the wild. Maybe Cam was correct when he said she had been missing out. There was something primal within her that thrilled to be a part of this most basic rite of nature.

Overhead an eagle soared and dipped, occasionally digging its talons in the stream to pull out a fish. She had seen eagles far away, but never one so close she saw each razor sharp talon as it extended to pierce its victim.

They stayed for hours, until the cold crept into her bones and made her numb. For a while, the bear crawled out of the water and napped on the bank before resuming his smorgasbord. Belle found it was as fascinating to watch the huge animal sleep as it was to watch him in action. How many people in the world got the chance to be so close to such a massive land predator and tell the tale?

"Do you think it would wake up if I went over and touched it?" she whispered.

Cam tightened his grip on her as if to keep her from finding out. "The fact that you would even ask that question is enough to give me nightmares," he murmured.

"It was theoretical. I wouldn't ever actually sneak up on a grizzly bear. Probably."

"If ever anyone would, it would be you," he said. His tone was longsuffering as if he were constantly plucking her out of danger.

"I'm not the one who watches grizzlies in my spare time for fun."

"You are now. Welcome to the club." And then, before she could reply, he kissed her. She returned his kiss wildly, still enough adrenaline pumping in her veins to make her reckless with passion. Cam seemed as lost as she was until he abruptly broke away and darted his eyes frantically toward the stream.

"Where did the bear go?" he asked, his careful tone stark contrast to the way his fingers now dug into her shoulders.

They froze, holding their combined breath, wondering if the bear had somehow gotten the drop on them while they were otherwise occupied. But they heard a telltale thrashing sound on the far side of the stream and relaxed.

"Let's go in case he got curious and is coming to inspect us," Cam said. He tossed her onto the horse and mounted behind her, turning the horse toward home.

As before, he walked the horse through the forest. When they reached the other side, he leaned down to whisper in her ear. "It's your call: run or walk."

"What do you think?" she asked.

With a cluck of Cam's tongue, the horse shot forward, jolting her backwards. Belle closed her eyes, flung her arms wide, and laughed all the way home.

CHAPTER 17

That night after supper, Cam and Belle sat cozily ensconced together on the porch swing, a downy blanket wrapped tightly around them. While the days were holding steady near fifty degrees, the nights were still freezing. It was too cold to be outside, but they were warm together under the blanket and too sleepy to move.

All in all, it had been a perfect day. Now, both drowsy from their lack of sleep the night before, they were perfectly content to sit and dangle lazily on the swing.

"I loved today," Belle whispered.

"Me, too," Cam murmured, lips nuzzling her ear.

She sat beside him, twisted toward him with her feet in his lap and her arms around his neck. He was performing another one of his bone melting foot massages on the ball of her right foot, and she was certain she would never find the energy to move again.

"We should work tomorrow," she whispered.

"Mmm, hmm." he said, absently grinding his thumb into her instep.

Right now she felt so utterly happy and peaceful she wanted to freeze this moment and make it last forever. Her hectic, frenzied life in New York seemed a million miles away. In an odd way, this Montana life felt brand new. Despite having grown up in there, she had never acclimated to the slow, small town pace. Before this moment, she had never understood the beauty of sitting still to watch a sunset. But then she had never had someone like Cam to share a sunset with. *Love makes all the difference,* she thought absently.

"Oh, oh no. No, no, no, no, no, no. *No,*" she exclaimed out loud. She sat bolt upright and gripped Cam by the shoulders. Her mouth worked frantically up and down, but no sound came out. For a horrified second, she thought she might be sick.

"What? What is it? Did you forget something? Did something bite you? What?" His eyes made a frantic search of her face.

"I'm in love with you," she blurted, the shock making her voice sound raw and hoarse.

He blinked a couple of times, relaxing slightly now that he knew there was no danger. "Well, yeah. I'm in love with you, too. I kind of thought it was a given. What's the big deal?"

What's the big deal? Had he really said that? Did he not realize the monumental shift that had occurred in her world? How on earth had she let this happen? How had everything spun out of control so far and so fast? How had she gone from playing catch up with an old friend/nemesis to never wanting to leave his side again? She had to get out of it, had to fix it, had to back away before something even worse happened.

Sensing her panic, he gripped her shoulders and looked deep into her eyes. "Belle, it's going to be okay."

"But, I, you…New York, and…How…"

"It's going to be okay," he reiterated. "It's love, not smallpox. Take a deep breath, baby."

She did as he instructed, breathing slowly in and out.

"Now kiss me like you mean it," he commanded.

"Don't think because I love you I'm going let you boss me around," she said. "But this once, I'm willing to make an exception and follow orders." With her hands still planted firmly on his shoulders, she leaned in and kissed him, and by the time she was finished, he had no doubt she meant it.

* * *

THE NEXT MORNING, Belle woke bright and early to get a quick start at the office. Of course Cam beat her there by two hours, but he didn't comment on it. She was relieved he didn't seem to expect her to rise as early as he did. She was used to getting up early in New York, but there was early and then there was *early*. By her calculation, he was up before five every morning. He usually worked a few hours on the ranch before retiring to the office to chip away at his never-ending paper trails.

They worked companionably together in his office for a couple of hours. He typed on the computer while she answered emails and returned messages. He was about to suggest they take a break when her line rang again. Since he was standing right next to the phone, he reached for it and answered with a smile.

"King Ranch, Belle Landry's office. How may I direct your call?" Then his expression lost all humor and turned arctic before he held the phone out to her.

"It's your boyfriend," he said, tone dripping acid.

She took the phone, instinctively backing away a step, as one does when confronted with angry, dangerous animals. "Hello," she answered, clearing her throat when it came up dry.

"Leave it to you to find a male secretary in Montana," Storm said, laughing. His jocular tone was sharp contrast to Cam's unblinking stare, now located six inches from her person.

"That's not my secretary. He owns the ranch and he's letting me share his office." She turned away from Cam's unwavering glare, staring at the wall opposite instead.

"Oh." His laughter dried up, as he read something unnatural in her tone. "That's nice of him, I suppose. But when I picture an office in Montana, it's always in somebody's garage."

"It's not."

"Oh." After his attempt at humor fell flat a second time, he wasn't sure where to go. "So how are you?"

"I'm good. How are you?"

"Still missing you." His tone was infused with warmth and affection, but there was no answering echo when she spoke.

"Storm, I should go." She didn't snap at him, but with Cam glaring at the back of her head, she was desperate to get off the line.

"Oh. Okay. Well, call me when you can. I'm still hoping you'll wrap this up quicker rather than later so you can get back to civilization. And to me," he added, only now he sounded sad and she felt bad about that. "Goodbye."

"Goodbye," she said. She pushed the button to end the call and stood staring once again at the misshapen wolf. "Did your mom take painting lessons?"

"No, she's a natural talent."

She didn't laugh in case he was serious. Some men thought their mothers could do no wrong. Plus his tone sucked the amusement right out of her.

"I was wondering why he's under the mistaken impression you two are still together?" Cam asked, his careful, controlled tone a warning for her to proceed with caution.

"I don't want to break up with him over the phone. That seems cruel."

"Which is crueler, to end it over the phone, or to leave him dangling while you spend your evenings in my arms?" he asked.

She blew out a breath and turned to scowl at him. "For a romance writer, you're not very romantic sometimes."

"Forgive me if I'm not in the mood to extend grace to the boyfriend of the woman I'm in love with," he said.

She grinned. "That's a little better. Fine. I'll make the call, but I'm taking it outside, and don't you dare try to listen in on another line." She jabbed her index finger at him for emphasis.

He held up his hands in surrender. "Wouldn't dream of it," he said, mentally crossing his fingers. He wanted to hear what she said to him and, since it was his phone, felt no compunctions about listening in.

But when she opened the door and strode outside, he saw Cade hovering outside the entrance to his office, frowning.

"What?" Cam asked.

"What was that part about you being a romance writer?"

Cam clenched his fist and tapped it on his thigh, aiming to calm his sudden rush of nerves. "Come in and shut the door behind you."

Cade did as instructed, his frown still firmly in place.

Cam waited to speak until they were fully situated, and then he blurted, "I wrote a story and it was published in a magazine."

If Cam had said he was having an operation to become a mermaid, Cade couldn't have been more surprised. "What?"

Instead of repeating what he had said, he continued with his story. "That's why Belle's here. She read the story in a magazine and tracked me down. She thought Layla was the writer at first. She wants to sell my book for me and represent me."

"What?" Cade repeated.

Cam sighed. "I wrote a book. I'm a writer. I write. Belle is going to be my agent. But I would prefer to keep this under my hat. I don't even want Coy, Ivy, Josh, or even Layla to know."

"*What?*" Cade said again, still disbelieving.

"Stop saying that. I know you heard me," Cam said.

"Of course I heard you," Cade said angrily. "I don't believe you. I don't believe that while I've been feeling bad for you busting your hump, always stuck in your office, you've actually been writing a book. I've been killing myself trying to help you get caught up."

Cam held up his hands in surrender. "I didn't start writing until you started helping me in the office. Before that, I was too swamped to attempt it. And I only write at night after you go to bed, so when you see me working during the day I really am working."

Cade didn't look any less angry, and a feeling of dread grew in the pit of Cam's stomach. This was the reaction he had feared. If his own brother reacted this badly, what could he expect from strangers? "Look," he began, but Cade interrupted him.

"I cannot believe all this time I've been trying to figure out how to get Layla not to be angry at me anymore, my own brother is a bona fide romance guru and hasn't helped me out. What were you thinking?"

Now it was Cam's turn to blink dazedly. "What?"

"She thinks I don't want to marry her. She can't understand why I won't propose. I've got to make a grand gesture, but I keep drawing a blank. I need help."

Cam rested his fingers under his chin and regarded his brother. "If it's grand you want, I've got an idea, but we have to hurry before Belle comes back."

* * *

OUTSIDE BELLE LEANED against the wall and closed her eyes. In theory, she knew she needed to break up with Storm. But she had never broken up with anyone before, and she wasn't looking forward to it now. Somehow she had always been the one who was broken up with.

You're too strong for me, Belle. Too pushy, too high maintenance, too standoffish, too busy, and the list went on. Seemingly she had been too much for everyone she had ever encountered until Storm. And Cam. How was it possible she was with both of them at once?

Was she doing the right thing? After all, Storm lived in New York with her. He liked and accepted her as she was. He had never once tried to change her. Instead, he appreciated about her the qualities that had caused other men to run away in terror.

But then there was Cam. She sneaked around the corner of the building and peeked at him through the window. He threw back his head and laughed at something Cade said, and her heart turned over in her chest. He was so…everything. Before she could lose her resolve, she went back to the front of the building and called Storm.

"It's me," she said with no preamble.

"Hey, what's up? Did you forget to tell me something?" She could tell he was smiling, and her heart broke a little bit. For that reason, she was more abrupt than she had intended to be.

"I want to break up."

Her proclamation was met with silence for almost a full minute.

"What?"

"I'm breaking up with you?"

"Why?"

"Because we're not right for each other. I think you need to find someone else, someone better suited for you," she said.

"We're perfect for each other," he countered. "I'm laid back when you're uptight. I'm artistic and you're all business. Things are good. Don't rock the boat because we're spending a couple of weeks apart."

"That's not why," she said.

"Then why?"

She made a fist and pressed it to her forehead, trying to think of a way to explain. "It's not working out," she said lamely.

"Don't do this, Belle. Don't go home and freak out on me. Whatever is going on there has nothing to do with us."

"You're right, it doesn't. I need for this to be over, Storm. I'm sorry."

"No. Until I see you and hear it from you in person, I refuse to accept it's over."

"I'm sorry you feel that way because watching me as I say it won't change the facts."

"Give it some time. Think about it."

"I've already thought about it. This is goodbye."

"It's not."

She growled in frustration. "It is."

"It's not."

She opened her mouth to argue again, but the phone was suddenly plucked from her fingers. Cam pressed the button to end the call. "It is," he said.

Belle wasn't sure whether to laugh in relief or cry in frustration. The absurdity of the situation hit her. Previously when she had lived here, no one wanted her. Now she was here again and caught between two men. The one she wanted was standing a few inches away, waiting for her to make a move.

She jumped, and he caught her. "It is," she said, and then she kissed him.

CHAPTER 18

That night Belle and Cam began the arduous task of revising his manuscript. Even though she had no intention of holding back her opinion, she was worried about his reaction to her suggestions. But she needn't have worried. He seemed to value and respect her input, responding well to her constructive criticism. At times, he argued with her over a change she wanted him to make and, occasionally, after making an impassioned plea, she changed her mind and agreed with him. After all, it was his book, and she wasn't an editor. She was simply someone with a lot of experience and a keen eye for the business; she knew what publishers were looking for.

They sat in the small den where they were guaranteed a measure of privacy. During one of the breaks, Belle stood to stretch her legs, noting a painting on the far wall.

You've got to be kidding me, she thought. *This can't be another wolf.*

But it was. This one had a short, blunt nose, almost like a snout. One ear was set high on its head and rounded like Mickey Mouse.

"Has your mother ever actually seen a wolf?" she asked.

"Hmm?" Cam looked up distractedly from the computer.

"Never mind," she muttered.

"We need to talk about something important," Cam said. He set the laptop aside and held out his hands to her.

She sat beside him, alarmed by his serious tone. "What?"

He took her hand and looked deep in her eyes. "Founder's Day."

She jerked her hand out of his clasp and flattened herself against the back of the couch. "I don't want to talk about it. Ever."

Slowly, he inched toward her, gently putting his arms around her and brushing his lips on her temple. "What happened to make you hate it so much?"

"Don't you remember?" she asked, softening slightly at his tender ministrations.

He shook his head. "Tell me," he urged.

And because it was Cam, she did. "It started when I was three. Actually, it might have started before then, only I don't remember. That year I became separated from my parents during the parade. Panicked, I thought I saw them across the street. I ran out in front of a float. The tractor driver didn't see me and ran over me. Luckily, I wasn't seriously hurt, but I had to spend the night in the hospital."

He hugged her tighter. "I'm so glad you're okay. You could have been killed." Even though he knew that memory must be traumatic, he didn't understand why she still held onto it. Then she started talking again.

"When I was five, I was on a float for my father's store. I fell off and knocked out my two front teeth. They were baby teeth, but because of the fall, I had to go to the hospital. Again.

"At seven I walked in the parade, twirling a baton. Long story short, a horse kicked me."

"I'm going to go out on a limb here and guess you wound up in the hospital."

She nodded, expression morose. "They remembered me. From that day on, I became labeled as 'The Founder's Day Accident Girl.'"

"But certainly you didn't have a medical emergency every year, did you? Why didn't you simply avoid the parade?"

"Oh, the parade episodes were the glory days of my youth. I think of them fondly in comparison to what came later. Things went downhill from there. At eleven, my father volunteered me to sing the national anthem."

"I didn't know you could sing."

"I can't. But it didn't matter because I was so nervous I only sang eight words before fading away and passing out. And of course I fell off the stage. When I came to, I begged them not to take me to the hospital. They didn't, but for months after that whenever people saw me they would sing, 'O say, can you see by the *darppp...*' and then pretend to pass out." She punched his arm. "It's not funny."

He shook his head, not trusting himself to speak. But tears of amusement sparkled on his lashes.

"Then the year I was thirteen, someone got sick and I became a last minute replacement at the dunking booth. It all happened so quickly, no one realized I was wearing a white t-shirt. And nothing underneath."

His jaw dropped. "That was you? If I remember correctly, my group of friends spent so much money taking turns we were responsible for re-roofing the library that year."

"If you remember it, how did you not know it was me?" she asked.

"I, ah, wasn't looking at your face." He paused and cleared his throat. "I can't believe that was you. I had dreams for months after that."

"That might explain why, the next year, Tony Parker kissed me behind the dunking booth."

"That doesn't sound traumatizing," he said.

"You didn't let me finish. It was my first kiss. His lip became stuck in my braces. We had to have his mom try and pull us apart. When she couldn't, I had to ride in the ambulance with him. He had to get three stitches. And of course, the hospital staffers remembered me."

"You're kidding. Don't those people ever retire?"

"One of them did. The nurses took my picture to send to one of the retired doctors for his birthday. They said he liked a good laugh since his wife died."

He put his hands over his face and groaned. "Please tell me that's the end."

"I wish I could. The year I turned sixteen, the news crew from Billings came to the parade, looking for a human-interest story. That's also the year I drove the tractor for the float. My thinking was it would be better to be in front than behind, less chance of getting run over again that way."

"Oh, no. This I remember." He gave her a sympathetic look as she continued.

"The footage of me losing control and plowing into the crowd from the senior center made national news."

"But it wasn't your fault the tire blew. The state patrol said so. And except for Mr. Whethers heart attack, no one was seriously injured," he said.

"Doesn't matter. For the rest of the school year, kids called me the Angel of Death."

His expression turned sheepish. "I may have come up with that one," he confessed.

"Cam," she exclaimed. "Mr. Whethers did not die."

"We were teasing you," he said soothingly. "Is that it? Is that the entire list?"

"No, there's one more," she said quietly.

"Tell me."

"The next year, my last, I decided I wasn't going to do anything. I didn't even want to go, but my parents made me. So I sat in the shade and watched, not saying a word to anyone. But it was hot that year, you remember?"

"I remember," he said. There had been a record crowd because of the unusual heat wave.

"I wanted something to drink. I wasn't paying attention to what they gave me, and neither were they."

"Don't tell me you drank the alcoholic version of the charity punch," he said.

"Seven cups. You know I don't drink. I was roaring drunk by the second cup. By the time I drank the seventh, I was out of my head."

"Is that it?"

She shook her head, looking miserable. "I saw Coy with Marissa. I wanted to get him alone, but I was too out of it to figure out a plan, so I ended up confessing the truth of my crush to both of them. Coy was sweet about it. He pressed his hand to my forehead and asked if I was okay. Marissa laughed and laughed."

To his surprise, she smiled a little. "What?"

"I threw up on her."

He laughed before picking her up, settling her in his lap, and cuddling her close.

She buried her face in his chest, seeking the comfort he offered. "When I sobered up, I was mortified. I think that was the final straw in my decision to move to New York. I didn't speak to Coy again, not even to say goodbye."

"He never told me about that," Cam mused.

"I'm sure he was as mortified as I was over it."

"I'm not sure anyone in history has ever been as mortified as you were," he said sympathetically.

"Now you see why I hate Founder's Day. Every time I so much as think about it, I see the people in the town laughing at me, always laughing at me."

When he realized she was crying silent tears, something inside him broke. He wanted to find anyone who had ever laughed at her and beat the stuffing out of them, himself included. Instead, he kissed her. Sometime later when they surfaced for air, he used his thumbs to wipe the last vestiges of her tears.

"You had no idea I was this pathetic, did you? Secretly crying over old wounds like a loser." She shook her head in disgust and ground her fist in her eye socket.

"I don't think you're pathetic or a loser. I think you had a lot of legitimately painful events. But, Belle, isn't it possible the memories are different for you than they are for everyone else? I was at every one of those Founder's Days, and I don't remember any of that stuff except for the tractor incident. And that was *funny*. Sometimes I still laugh when I think of old Mrs. Carter using her walker to trip the people who got in her way. And, yes, we were all frightened when Mr. Whethers dropped, but, Sweetheart, he weighed almost four hundred pounds and used bacon as a condiment. If I remember correctly, he was eating pork rinds when you hit him."

She giggled, surprised she could actually laugh over his exaggerations. "You also remember the dunk tank incident," she said.

"Yes, I do," he said solemnly. "And it remains as one of my fondest memories. It was the first time I realized what made girls so interesting. All in all, it was a highly educational and profound experience. And now that I know it was you, well, let's say there's a good chance the dreams will start again."

She laughed again, pressing her palms to her overheated cheeks. "You stop that. I'm blushing."

"I feel a little flushed myself." He smiled at her and smoothed the hair off her wet face.

"I suppose it's possible I remember the events more clearly than some people. And Coy didn't seem to hold on to any awkwardness over my confession."

Cam scowled. "That's the only part of the story that bothers me. Why did you have to love my brother first?"

Now it was her turn to comfort him. "I didn't love Coy. I thought I did because, except for my parents, he was the only kindness in my teenage life."

"I should have been a better friend to you," Cam said regretfully.

"You should have been exactly as you were. Sometimes you drove me crazy, but I always liked and respected you," she said. "You drove me to excel, so be better at everything, if only to beat you."

He grinned. "I liked you, too. You could always make me laugh, and I enjoyed competing with you."

"Want to know the best part?" she asked.

He nodded.

"I didn't throw up on anyone when I told you I loved you."

"That's not the best part," he said. "The best part is that I love you back."

"Aw, Cam, I'm not sure how long it's going to take me to get used to hearing sweet things from you."

Give it time, he thought. *I'm planning on forever with you.*

CHAPTER 19

The next day Belle agreed to spend the day working the ranch with Cam, like a real rancher. At the time it had sounded almost fun, and then four thirty rolled around and she realized she was crazy for agreeing to anything that got her out of bed before the sun came up.

However, when Cam tiptoed into Layla's room to wake Belle with a gentle kiss, she decided there were worse things than getting up early. He tried to stand upright, but her arms clung, pulling him back for another kiss.

"Let's go before we wake Layla," he muttered against Belle's ear. He extricated himself from her embrace and eased out of the room.

"That ship has sailed," Layla said when he was gone. "Here's a tip: it's not possible to kiss like that and not wake the person next to you."

"Sorry," Belle said sheepishly, genuinely embarrassed by her sleep-numbed actions.

"I'm teasing you," Layla said, sounding a little too cheerful for so early in the morning. "It's almost my normal wakeup time anyway. Maybe I'll go see what Cade's up to."

The two women shared a smile before Belle peeled herself out of bed and began dressing. It took longer than normal because her brain was still sleep-addled. "How long did it take you to get used to getting up this early?"

"Not long," Layla said. "But then I've always been a morning person. I was a foster kid. It was never a good idea to be the last one still sleeping."

Belle's hand froze on her button. "I didn't know that. Cam said you came here as part of the witness protection program."

"I did. I had just graduated from the system and had nowhere else to go. Sad and scary as it was, witnessing that murder saved my life. Here I've found a home and a family."

"So you're happy here," Belle said. Sometimes she wasn't sure.

"I am," Layla said with conviction. "In addition to being in love with Cade, I really love this family like they're my own. The other guys feel like true brothers to me. And the community has adopted me, too. I never knew what it meant to have roots before."

"I'm not sure I know, either, and I'm from here," Belle said.

"We could be your family, if you let us," Layla said softly, gently.

For some reason the loving words so gently spoken brought tears to Belle's eyes. "I'm very confused, Layla," she confessed for the first time. She dropped all pretense of trying to dress, sitting back down on the bed instead. "I'm beginning to feel torn in two. I love my life in New York, but I can't imagine leaving Cam in a couple of days."

"If he's really important to you, something will work out. Cade accuses me of being an optimist, but I think I'm more of a fatalist. If it's meant to be, it will be," Layla said.

Belle smiled at her. "I like watching you and Cade together. You give me hope there actually can be a happy ending in the world."

Layla's smile slipped slightly. "To be honest, I feel like a failure lately in that department. Before Coy and Ivy were married, I was happy with the way things were. I mean, Cade and I got together when we were only eighteen. I wasn't looking for marriage yet. But now, seeing what a difference marriage makes, I want that. I'm not sure Cade does."

"You didn't know Cade before," Belle said. "He was a rounder, two years younger and still notorious. That kid had more swagger than all the other King brothers put together. I was older and out of his realm, so he always treated me with a sort of brotherly deference, but the other girls in his path were used up and tossed away like tissues. Believe me when I tell you he's in love with you in a forever kind of way. He's not the same guy he was before. But knowing people here the way I do, I can guess he's still having some issues with his disability. Here, it's all about male pride. They like to be the caregivers and providers. My guess is Cade is still finding his way in that department. I know it's unsolicited advice, but be patient with him."

"I have no choice. I love him," Layla said.

"You always have a choice," Belle replied. "I wasn't kidding when I said you can do anything you set your mind to. You could go anywhere, be anything."

"I don't want to go anywhere else; this is my home. But I would like to talk to you about my options," Layla said, sounding shy.

"Fire away," Belle said, settling back against the headboard. But before Layla could get started, there was a knock at the door.

"Belle, you have thirty seconds before I come in there and finish dressing you myself," Cam said. He must have heard their voices through the door and knew Layla was awake.

"Threaten me again, and I'll reenact the dunk tank for everyone but you," she said.

There was a pause before he spoke again. "Just hurry please," he said, his tone suddenly deferential.

She rolled her eyes at Layla. "Men. I guess I'd better go. We'll talk later, I promise."

"Okay," Layla said, smiling sweetly. "Have fun today."

Belle paused by the door, turning back. "Have you ever worked cattle with them?"

Layla shook her head. "I wouldn't go without Cade. But if their laundry is any indication, I can tell you you're in for a busy day."

"Yippee," Belle muttered. She left the bedroom and went to the kitchen where Cam was waiting impatiently. "I'm ready."

"Eat something," he commanded.

"You said we're in a hurry."

"We are, but you need to eat. It's going to be a long day."

"Okay," she agreed. She drank a small glass of milk and grabbed one of Layla's oatmeal cookies on her way out the door.

"That's not much food," he commented.

"I'm only one small girl, and I have a figure to maintain."

"You'll maintain it today, trust me," he said. He draped his arm over her shoulders as they walked outside. Coy, Josh, and a couple of their ranch hands were already in their saddles.

"Oh, everyone really was waiting on me. I thought you were being impatient."

"When am I ever impatient?" he asked with mock innocence.

She gave him a look before turning to address the waiting cowboys. "I'm sorry, everyone. I guess I'm still on New York time."

"It's no problem," Coy assured her. "We're hoping that with you here today, Cam won't be as much of an iron fist as usual."

"Think again," Cam said. He tossed Belle gently into the saddle and swung up behind her.

"We're not taking the black horse today?" she asked, disappointed.

"No, he's no good for working cattle. Think of the horses like cars. The stallion is like a convertible sports car. This one," he paused to pat the white and brown horse beneath him, "is like a reliable Ford. Those," he pointed to some draft horses in the pasture, "are like four wheel drive SUV's."

She pointed to a couple of sleek-looking horses in their own enclosure. "What about those?"

"Those are Ivy's. They're the cream of the crop—think of an expensive, rare European car everyone in the world dreams of owning. Her father gave her those as a wedding present to help start her breeding business. The lineage on those horses can be traced back to European royalty hundreds of years ago."

Belle whistled. "They must cost a fortune."

"They do, and Ivy's been making good use of them. She has clients from as far away as California coming here for stud services."

Belle snickered.

"Grow up, Landry," Cam said, but he was laughing too.

"I guess when I think about ranching, I think you raise cows and sell them, but there are a lot of details to think about."

"That there are," he agreed. "There's parentage, growth, feed, medicine, pastures, fires, water, cowhands, the government…" He released a sigh. "The list is endless. And don't even get me started on Wall Street."

"What does Wall Street have to do with the ranch?"

"Everything. Commodity trading determines how much we'll get for our beef. Since biofuel became a buzzword, corn prices went through the roof."

"Why does corn affect you? I thought the cows grazed all day."

"They do, during good weather. But you know what our winters are like. We supplement with corn, hay, and other grains. The business isn't static. It changes every year, depending on the government, the economy, the weather. Even changing whims of people and their diets. Right now it's trendy to blame us for global warming, as if our cows emit more methane than all the millions of cars, buses, and factories in the city. Everything depends on everything else. It's all connected."

"Hmm." She was strangely humbled by this new information. His job was much harder and more stressful than she ever realized. And in a way, he was providing a much-needed service for the country. Who else kept everyone fed but farmers and ranchers?

The morning air was frosty. Before her, she saw her breath and Cam's as it puffed out beside her. Beyond the peaceful snuffling of the horses, there was no other sound. The sun hadn't come up yet. The only signal others were with them was an occasional glint of moonlight from a belt buckle, making it feel like she and Cam were alone in the world. The peace of the moment went deep and settled somewhere inside her, smoothing over her rough patches. She knew when she went back to New York and became overwhelmed by the hectic pace of her life, this was the moment she would come back to; the moment where all the world was still asleep and she was awake, helping to perpetuate the circle of life.

"What are you thinking?" Cam whispered. She wondered if he was alarmed by her unnatural silence.

"Deep thoughts," she said, vaguely embarrassed she was so touched by the silent scene. "What are we doing today?"

"Moving cattle from one pasture to another so we can do some fence repairs," he said.

"It takes all these men to move cattle?"

"You'll see," he said cryptically.

She shifted in the saddle, anxious to arrive and get started. So far she was fascinated by everything she had witnessed on the ranch. She had the feeling today would be no exception. A short while later, the lowing of cattle alerted her to the fact that they were getting close.

"Look there," Cam said. He nudged her toward the eastern horizon. The sun was starting to rise. It looked huge, as if it were going to swallow the earth. Cam kept the horse moving slowly toward their destination, but it did nothing to stop her from taking in the full view.

"The last time I watched the sun rise was four years ago in Manhattan. My roommate, Ruth, and I went up on our rooftop and watched the sun peek over Central Park."

"That sounds nice," he said, his thumb sliding slowly around her hipbone.

She was glad he didn't press her to choose which one she liked better; it was the same sun, and they were both beautiful.

"Cam, will you come to New York sometime?" she asked.

He paused for so long, she was certain he would say no. "I'll have to sign a contract with you, won't I?"

"Yes."

"I'll go for that. I can see where you work and live. It'll be fun."

She tilted back in the saddle so she could smile up at him. "That's a great idea."

"It's a good time to go before the ranch heats up. Spring and summer are busy around here."

Her smile turned sad. "Isn't it always busy around here?"

"It is," he agreed with a sigh. His arm tightened around her. With effort, she pushed away the melancholy that threatened to consume her. Maybe all they had was right now, and for that reason she determined to enjoy it.

They were almost at their destination when one of the cowboys circled back and rode over to Cam.

"We've got a buck tangled in a fence up ahead, boss. Which one of us do you want to handle it?"

"Stay with me and we'll go," Cam said. He relayed the message to Coy. He and the other cowboys banked right while Cam, Belle and the cowhand banked left.

When they neared the fence, Belle saw a large buck with a full rack suspended in barbed wire. At first, she thought it was dead, but she soon realized it was resting. As they approached, it began to furiously kick with all four legs, but only managed to entangle itself further.

"Does this happen often?" she asked.

"Occasionally. Either they don't see the fence, or think they can make it. Sometimes it starts with their antlers getting caught, but you can see how they make it worse by panicking." He frowned. "I shouldn't have brought you. This isn't going to be pretty."

"It's okay," she said, trying to sound brave. "I can handle it. I'm here to get the full ranch picture today."

Absently, he patted her thigh and reined the horse to a stop. "Do you want to come with us or stay on the horse?" he asked after he dismounted.

Belle looked down, saw the ground so far below the tall horse, and quickly made up her mind. "I'll go with you."

He lifted his hands and pulled her down. They walked to the buck, but Belle kept a safe distance as she watched Cam and the cowboy study the deer, trying to figure the best way to get it unstuck.

"Can you grab the wire cutters from my bag?" Cam asked the cowboy who Belle now realized was Tanner. He grinned at her as he passed, and she tried not to feel embarrassed by their almost kiss. Had that only been a few days ago?

Tanner returned the tool to Cam. "Want me to shoot it, boss?" he asked, sounding a little too eager.

"No, I only have my rifle. I think…" He paused and turned to look at Belle. "Maybe you should turn around, Sweet."

"I want to see what happens," she said and meant it. This was the gory side of country life she hadn't given much thought to. What happened when things went wrong and not everything looked like a picture on a postcard?

Cam nodded and turned back to the animal. "There's no way to untangle it. With all that wire cutting through its stomach, it wouldn't live anyway. Better to put it out of its misery." She wondered if he was giving the speech for her benefit, trying to explain to her what he was about to do. He pulled a wicked looking knife from his belt. "Tanner, I'm going to hold its antlers. You do the rest."

Belle knew better than to protest, but she wanted to. Not for the buck, its life was over the moment it became tangled in the wire. But its rack was huge and it was panicked, thrashing to and fro. Even caught in the wire it was a powerful animal. There was the distinct possibility Cam could get hurt. Her fists clenched at her sides, she had to will herself not to look away.

"On my count," Cam said. "Ready, set, now." Plunging his hands into the tangled wire, he grabbed the beast by the antlers while Tanner also stuck his hand into the fray. As she had feared, the buck increased its thrashing. The only sound coming from Cam was a grunt of exertion as he tried to hold the animal still. At last, Tanner was able to reach the neck. He neatly slit the deer's throat. It continued to thrash, spraying the men with blood until at last death caught up with it.

Tanner neatly extracted his hands without a scrape, but Cam wasn't so lucky. He remained with his hands gripping the antlers. When Belle saw the blood, she ran forward, but he yelled for her to stop.

"Stay back. This is sharp wire."

"But you're injured. I need to get you out."

"You can't do it without gloves. Tanner will get me out."

She was thankful for the thick leather gloves they wore. Even though they obviously hadn't protected Cam from getting hurt, they allowed Tanner to pick his way around the barbs enough to extract Cam's arms.

At last he was free. But before he would allow her to see to his wounds, he and Tanner had to free the deer. Working together, they untangled the deer from the wire. It dropped heavily to the earth. Tanner dragged it away from the fence.

"We'll have to add that to our list of repairs," Cam said. He walked to Belle and held his arms out for inspection. She gingerly took them in her hands and looked at them. They had been shredded by the wire, but the cuts didn't look deep. However, there was a long gash on his arm that was oozing blood. He noticed her concerned stare.

"Deer caught me with an antler," he explained.

"Let's go back to the house and I'll get you cleaned up."

He gave her a patronizing smile. "We don't have to go back to the house. There's a first aid kit in my saddle bag."

"But, Cam, you're hurt."

"Sweetheart, this is nothing," he said.

"Boss is right," Tanner said. "This one time I…"

Cam cut him off with a shake of his head. "Not helpful. She's a city girl. Let's not scare her any more than necessary. You can go on ahead; we'll catch up in a few minutes."

"Sure thing," Tanner said easily. He swung up into his saddle and took off.

"Everyone seems so laid back here," she noted as she watched him ride away.

"In a way, you have to be. The job changes every day. If you're not the type of person who can go with the flow and adapt, you're in the wrong profession. Plus worrying is my job. He gets paid to do as he's told, not to make the decisions." While he talked, he unbuttoned his shirt and took it off. "Do you mind playing doctor with me?" To make sure she was thoroughly flustered, he winked at her.

Without answering, she bustled to retrieve the medical kit from his saddlebag. "Is there somewhere you can sit?" she asked. "You're very tall."

They were in a pasture with no fallen trees so he sat on the ground. It must have been damp and cold, but he didn't complain. Belle sifted through the emergency kit to find cleaning solution and began to gently clean his wounds. She had never pictured herself as the Florence Nightingale type, patiently administering to some man's needs. But with Cam she found she rather enjoyed salving his wounds. Though the notion was old-fashioned, she enjoyed the nurturing side of her that tending to him revealed.

Whatever was in the solution must have stung because he grimaced. The cuts on his hand were numerous and shallow. It was the gash on his forearm that worried her. "This is deep, Cam."

He flexed his hand a few times. "I don't think it hit muscle. It's fine."

"You need stitches."

"If I do, one of the men can patch me up later."

She put her hands on her hips. "Cameron King, this is the twenty first century. You cannot have a cowboy sew up your arm. You could get gangrene."

He grinned up at her. "You're so cute when you're indignant, Belle. One of our hands was a medic in the army. He has a medical kit, and he knows what he's doing. I don't want to make an all day trip into the city for a couple of stitches."

She couldn't argue with his logic, but she didn't have to like it. Huffily, she finished cleaning his wounds, dressing the arm gash as best she could. He sat smiling up at her while she worked.

"What?" she asked.

"You're much better at dressing my wounds than I am. It's nice."

She leaned down to place a kiss on the top of his head. "A better solution would be to not get injured in the first place."

"You worried about me, Belle?"

"I will be now that I know what can happen. I mean, you were lucky to get off as easily as you did." She shuddered, remembering how the wire had chewed up the deer's body.

"You could just as easily fall off the subway platform or get hit by a cab. Accidents can happen anywhere," he pointed out.

"Don't be reasonable when I'm feeling irrational, Cam. It's annoying."

Laughing, he took the emergency kit from her and secured it in his saddlebag before retrieving the shirt he had tossed over the horse.

"Wait," she said before he could put it on.

"What?" he asked.

"I haven't checked you for ticks yet. You were sitting in the tall grass. I should look, don't you think?"

Without waiting for an answer, she ran her hands gently over his chest, then walked behind him to give his back the same treatment before returning to the front.

"Am I all clear?" he asked, secretly wondering if she might need therapy for her tick preoccupation.

"Oh, you're good," she said. "You're perfect." He gave his chest one final poke and pat, for good measure.

He stood still while she pulled on his shirt and buttoned it for him. "I'm tempted to get injured more often if this is the treatment I get," he said.

"Better make it good. I'm not going to fly thousands of miles for cuts and bruises," she said.

A vague, "We'll see," kept her wondering what he meant as he settled them into the saddle and took off.

CHAPTER 20

The next morning, Belle was thankful she hadn't agreed to work cattle again. The previous day had been exhausting, yet fulfilling. After she finished cleaning Cam's wounds, they joined up with the other cowboys who had already started rounding up the cattle. Upon their arrival she noticed for the first time the two dogs barking and snapping at the cow's heels.

"Australian cattle dogs," Cam explained in her ear. "See how they're trained to respond to Josh's whistles? They're his pet project and, I have to say, I've been amazed by how much they help."

"You're a team player, Cam," she said. She had always thought of him as being autocratic, but he wasn't. Maybe he had the final say on things, but he was fair, willing to take input from his brothers and employees.

"Want to join my team?" His flippant tone did nothing to hide the seriousness behind the question. In response, she gave him an enigmatic smile. "That's not a no," he said hopefully. With a cluck of his tongue, they shot forward and joined the fray, urging the confused mass of cows into action. The cows, being herd animals, would choose a leader and follow it, no matter where it went. For that reason, little sects of cows continually tried to break off and go their own direction. That was why there were so many cowboys and dogs, to control the stragglers and keep the sprawling herd from splintering.

Occasionally, a lone cow would sneak out of the shuffle and sprint away. More than once she saw a cowboy throw a lasso and drag it back.

"Cowboys really do use lassos," Belle whispered, more to herself than Cam. He heard her anyway and chuckled quietly to himself.

"My little city slicker," he said, giving her waist a light squeeze.

It was true; she might as well have grown up in Manhattan for all she knew of her home state. Even though their town was tiny, she hadn't ventured out of it much. A few times she had come to the ranch at Coy's invitation, but they usually swam or played in one of the barns, never venturing far onto the ranch. A couple of times he had tried to get her to ride horses with him, but both times had ended in her falling off, much to Cam's amusement. Now, seeing the underbelly of the ranch up close and in person was like entering a whole new world. She began to think that though she was the one who had left home for the big city, she was actually the one who was sheltered and inexperienced. Living here his whole life had given Cam wisdom and experience beyond his years. He'd had to grow up fast, making adult decisions as soon as he took over the ranch for his father at the age of nineteen.

They had eaten lunch while they worked, nibbling on beef jerky and crackers while they sat in the saddle. Belle had felt both authentic as a cowgirl and ravenous when she returned home. Layla's huge meals were beginning to make sense. If the men were as hungry as she was, it was a wonder they could keep enough food on the premises to feed them every day.

But that was yesterday. Today, Cam had given her the morning off while he worked with the men repairing the fence from yesterday. He told her to sleep in, and she did. She woke at nine, stiff, sore, and patting her aching backside with a grimace. Long stretches in the saddle weren't for the fainthearted.

After showering and putting on her makeup, she left in search of sustenance. Even though she had eaten more than she thought possible last night, some lingering hunger pangs remained. Coffee wouldn't be enough this morning; she wanted food. Layla, in her wisdom after having lived here so long, had reserved a large portion of French toast for Belle. "Layla, have I told you lately I love you?" Belle asked.

"Not since last night at dinner," Layla said. She poured coffee for herself and Belle before sitting down across from her at the table.

"I feel ridiculously slothful," Belle said after her first bite of the delicious toast. "I slept late in your bed and now I'm lazing around eating your food."

"You're on vacation," Layla replied. "Something tells me you don't get a lot of downtime in New York."

"Never," Belle said, not realizing how weary she sounded. "I work eighteen hour days almost every day."

"That sounds exhausting."

Belle opened her mouth to say how much she loved her job, but stopped short. "It is. I think I need to find some balance when I go back. It's easy to get caught up in the rat race, you know? Everyone is trying to be the best and get ahead. Without someone to keep me reined in, I can easily become a workaholic."

Layla nodded as if she understood, but she didn't. She had only ever had one job, and she was doing it now. While it was sometimes hard work, she never had a deadline and she had no one to compete with. "I've been dying to talk to you," Layla began.

Belle hesitated. Layla sounded like someone who was about to confess a horrible secret. Was she leaving the ranch after all? Cam would never forgive her if he thought she had encouraged the younger girl to leave. "What about?"

"My dream. You said you knew about my hobby and you thought I should go for it."

Belle nodded, not revealing she had been talking about writing at the time. She was a big believer in following dreams, no matter what they were, and she was curious to hear Layla's. "I misspoke when I said I knew what your dream was. I don't think I do. Why don't you tell me?"

Layla bit her lip. "I'm afraid you'll think it's stupid."

"Never," Belle said vehemently, then paused. "Unless it's becoming a representative for Mrs. King's artwork. That woman needs to put down the paintbrush."

Layla burst out laughing and quickly put her hands over her mouth. "I know, aren't they awful? And you've only seen the wolf ones. I've been surreptitiously tucking them into more out of the way places as I've run across them."

"You mean there are more?"

"Remind me to show you the series she did on the brothers."

Belle squeezed her eyes shut and shook her head. "Oh, sweet mercy. The horror."

"One of them is brown. I don't know why, and I don't know which brother it's supposed to be." Layla giggled again. "I shouldn't be telling you this. She's so sweet."

"Our secret," Belle said. "Now what's your dream?"

"Candy," Layla said.

"Candy?" Belle repeated, not understanding.

"Candy. I've been experimenting with a huckleberry caramel recipe. Caramels are hot right now, and huckleberries always sell well. I think it's a unique niche in a market that's barely been tapped."

"Hmm." Belle leaned back to study her. It sounded as if she had given the idea a lot of thought and not as if she was jumping into something because she liked to make caramel. "I'll tell you what. Make up a batch for me to taste, and I'll see what I can do to get the ball rolling. But I think you know me well enough by now to realize I'm going to be brutally honest in my opinion. Don't get me involved if you don't want to hear it."

"I want to," Layla said. "You're a professional businesswoman. I've spent hours going over this plan in my head, but I don't have the confidence or know how to get it started. You do. I'll be glad for whatever help you can give me." She jumped up and began clattering pots and pans. "It will only take a couple of hours."

"Sounds good. I'll go get some work done in the office. Come get me when you're ready."

Layla paused in her preparations. "Thanks, Belle."

"I'm glad to help," Belle said. "Honestly and tremendously. Women with a dream need to stick together. I would tell Ivy the same thing, but I'm afraid of what she would want me to do with the horses."

She left Layla laughing and went to the office to work. Two hours later, Layla knocked tentatively on the door. "You don't have to knock," Belle said. "It's not my office. But come in anyway."

Layla stepped inside, set a platter on the table and backed away as if she were a servant offering food to a king. Her deferential attitude bothered Belle, but she took her nerves into account and spared her a lecture on confidence.

Holding the candy in her palm, she turned it over and over to inspect it. It was a pretty purple rectangle—slightly darker than huckleberries and wrapped in plain wax paper. So far, it passed the appearance test. Next she had to taste it. She popped it in her mouth and chewed slowly, enjoying the smooth chewiness of the candy. The tartness of the huckleberries was a perfect complement to the sweetness of the caramel.

"I'm not a hyperbolic person," Belle said when she was finished. "But that was awesome. I can't believe you invented that recipe." Layla beamed at her. "And now I have a question for you. How big do you want to be?"

"I...I guess I want to be able to support myself if I need to. I want to contribute more here than clean floors. I want to contribute financially."

"Sounds good," Belle said. "I'm going to make some calls. I'll come back to the house when I'm finished to let you know how it went."

"O-okay," Layla stammered, taken aback by how quickly things were progressing. "Thank you."

"Sure," Belle said absently. She pulled out her phone and began to scroll through a list of numbers.

When she returned to the house over an hour later, Layla was sitting at the kitchen table, her hands clasped nervously in her lap.

Belle sat down across from her. "I have some exciting news. I talked to my dad. He's going to start selling your candy in his store. The final cost will be between the two of you, but he's fair and knowledgeable about that sort of thing."

"Really?" Layla asked excitedly. "That's so great. I can't believe this."

Belle laughed. "That's not the exciting news I was referring to. The husband of one of my clients is a buyer for a major grocery chain. Apparently your market research was spot on because he was ecstatic over the idea, although he's located on the east coast. He said it would be cost prohibitive at this point to ship the candy that far."

"Oh," Layla said, biting back her disappointment. Still, someone important had liked her idea. That was encouraging.

"Okay, you're going to have to stop reacting until I finish saying everything. Your big brown eyes make me feel like I'm conversing with a puppy. My contact put me in contact with a west coast buyer." She paused to smile. "He was equally enthused about the idea. He wants a thousand units of your product by next week. He'll start testing them then. If they sell well, he'll put them in stores up and down the west coast and in Canada."

Layla blinked at her, unspeaking. Belle didn't know if she was in shock or simply following orders.

"Because I realize that's too much for any one person to accomplish in such a short amount of time, I also called my mother. She and some of her friends from church will be here as soon as you call them with a time. By her calculation, it would take six workers, but she said she could get more if you wanted. They'll work pro bono for now, but if it works out you can pay them then. I also did some checking on a commercial kitchen. The Presbyterian church in town has a large commercial kitchen that has already been approved by the health department. They're going to rent it to you for a nominal fee whenever you want for as long as you want." She paused. "You can talk now."

Instead of talking, though, Layla burst into tears and ran from the house.

"That was unexpected," Belle said, not really sure what to do with herself. "I guess I'll go back to work," she said to no one. Because she had spent the afternoon working on Layla's candy, she had barely scratched the surface of her own work.

As she approached the office, Layla stepped out, wiping her eyes. "I'm sorry I ran out like that," Layla said. "It belatedly occurred to me I hadn't told Cade anything about what was going on, and I wanted to make sure and tell him before he heard it from anyone else."

"That's no prob…" Belle started, but Layla cut her off by throwing her arms around her waist and laying her head on her shoulder.

"Thanks, Belle. You have no idea how much this means to me."

Belle returned her hug. "I do, actually. My boss gave me a job my first day in New York, and it was a dream come true. I'm paying it forward. Someday you'll have the opportunity to help some other woman with a dream."

Layla let her go and stepped back, her eyes twinkling. "You're right. I'm going to go right now and call those galleries in Billings to see if I can get them to display some of Mrs. King's work."

"Naughty. I'm going to tell her you said that." Layla's eyes rounded with panic and Belle laughed. "Kidding."

Layla laughed. "I need to go make a list and then go to bed because I have a feeling this is the last night I'll be sleeping for a long time." She gave Belle a happy little wave before turning to walk toward the house.

Belle's smile faded when she walked into the office and saw Cade staring out the window. He turned and offered her a weak smile.

"Layla told me all you did for her this afternoon. Thank you."

She walked over to him and took the seat across from his desk. "I'm not convinced you're thrilled."

"I am, in theory. But change is hard and scary, you know? I guess I wish what she already has could be enough for her."

Meaning that he wished *he* could be enough for her. "Have you ever studied Maslow's hierarchy of needs?" she asked, throwing him off guard.

"Unless that's some sort of cattle-breeding theory or football play then no."

"It's one of the only things I remember from my college psychology class. It states that we seek our most primary needs first, like food, shelter, water. When those are fulfilled we seek love and belonging. After that comes things that are closer to our core, like purpose and esteem. I guess what I'm trying to say is the fact that Layla feels comfortable enough to pursue her dreams is a sign of how well you're doing. By providing for her needs and loving her, you're giving her the ability to pursue her desires. She's blossoming, Cade, and it's thanks to you. You shouldn't be threatened by her success; you should be gratified."

"I certainly never would have thought of it that way. But maybe you're right. When she first came here, she was so uncertain of her place we had to convince her to stay. I had to go to Chicago and practically drag her back here. But now, not only does she want to be here, but she feels comfortable enough to start a risky business." He was talking mostly to himself, trying to puzzle things together and make up his mind about them.

She started to stand, thinking maybe he was ready to be alone. But he reached over the table and caught her hand. "Belle, I can't tell you how happy I am to have you here. The changes I've seen in Cam are … And I know about the book. I think it's great."

"Who would have guessed Cam was such a sweetheart under that serious exterior?"

"I'm not sure I would have used the word sweetheart, but I knew there were hidden depths of greatness to my brother. He did a lot to get me back on my feet after the accident, metaphorically speaking. He's a great guy."

"You're preaching to the choir," she said.

"So what happens when you leave here?" he asked.

"That's the million dollar question, and I'm doing my best not to think about it."

He smiled. "If I know Cam, he's doing enough thinking for the both of you." It would be interesting to see which of them came out the victor in their no win situation—Cam, who wouldn't leave Montana without dynamite as a motivating factor, or Belle who seemed equally as adamant about staying in New York. "Belle, there's one more thing. I want to tell you something I've learned since Layla came into my life. No matter what the cost, love is worth the price."

"I'll keep that in mind," Belle said.

"See that you do," Cade said, and because his bossy, serious tone sounded so much like Cam, she laughed.

CHAPTER 21

The next night Belle's parents came for supper. While Belle helped Layla in the kitchen, Cam loaded the elder Landrys in the all terrain-looking golf cart and took them on an abbreviated tour of the ranch. They arrived back at the house thoroughly awed and impressed by the spread. Her father was talking a mile a minute about bulls, stocks, neighbors, and his store. Cam listened with attentive patience that unknowingly won points with Belle. Since she had inherited her father's single-minded, chatty nature, she knew many people found it annoying. She caught his eye and smiled at him across the room. He winked in return.

Her mother, from whom Belle had inherited her eagle-eyed powers of observation, did not miss the exchange. She practically preened in satisfaction over what she saw developing between her only child and the area's wealthiest rancher.

Belle was both pleased and exasperated by the action. While she and her mother got along, their relationship was a precarious one. Mostly because her mother undulated from wanting Belle to follow her dreams and be a successful career woman to wanting her to get married and have babies. Lately, the pendulum seemed to have swung more toward the marriage/baby side of things. And, though she hadn't met him, she hadn't approved of Storm. There was no doubt in anyone's mind she approved of Cam.

The large kitchen was crowded with so many people gathered around the table that night. Conversation buzzed as her father attempted to chat up everyone in the room. Layla and Belle's mother talked about their upcoming candy workday. Ivy and Coy were lost in their own little newlywed world while Cade and Josh were attempting to answer her father's questions about cattle.

"You look happy," Cam spoke softly in Belle's ear.

"I am," she said. Being an only child with few cousins, she wasn't accustomed to large family gatherings, but she found she liked it. There was a pervading sense of love floating around the room, leaving Belle feeling slightly euphoric. "I keep thinking I want to freeze a moment because there will never be another like it; then a new one comes along to top the old one. I'm having so much fun here, Cam."

"That's good because sometime soon we need to have a talk, Belle. About us."

She swallowed down a lump of panic and nodded. *Please don't ask me to stay,* she mentally pled with him. Much as she loved him, and as much as she was enjoying his home and family, she wasn't ready to give up her career or life in New York.

There was a tap on the door, almost too faint to hear over the din of conversation. "I'll get it, y'all sit still," Ivy announced. She bounded to the living room and returned a few minutes later. "Belle, it's for you."

Belle didn't understand the tension in her tone until she turned and saw Storm standing a foot behind Ivy and looking sullen. All conversation came to an abrupt halt as nine pairs of eyes slowly bounced between Belle and Storm.

For possibly the first time in her life, Belle was absolutely speechless and had no idea what to do. She sat staring at Storm with her mouth open and no sound coming out. Finally Cam stood, knocking over his chair in the process. He bent over to retrieve it, and then he spoke.

"You've come a long way. Sit down and have supper with us."

Startled into action by Cam's invitation, everyone on Belle's side of the table slid down the long bench, making way for Storm. He squeezed in beside her without a word or glance, which was good because Belle was still thunderstruck.

Cam sat on Belle's other side, looked to her to make the introduction, realized she was still wordless, and reached around her. "I'm Cameron King. This is our ranch. Welcome. These are Belle's parents, Mr. and Mrs. Landry, my brother Coy, his wife, Ivy, my brother Josh, my brother Cade, and his girlfriend Layla."

"I'm Storm McCay," Storm said. He looked dazed. Belle wasn't sure if it was from the trip or the culture shock. As far as she knew, Storm had only left New York to go to Europe for art school. Belle felt for him. He was out of his element, and he was obviously distraught over their breakup. But pity did nothing to help her find her voice. In fact, it had the disheartening effect of causing tears to spring to her eyes.

"Excuse me," she choked.

Storm and Cam jerked their heads up at the same time, watching her leave and ready to go after her. But her mother beat them to it.

"I'll go check on her," she announced. "Please go ahead and eat without us."

Belle made it as far as the hallway where she turned toward the wall and pressed her forehead against it. Perhaps it wasn't the most ladylike pose, but the cool plaster felt heavenly on her flushed forehead.

"Belle," her mom said, snapping Belle to attention.

"I don't know what to do, Mom," Belle said shakily. "I've hurt Storm, I'm going to continue to hurt him, and I never wanted that. This is a disaster. What am I going to do?"

"You're going to go back in there and display as much grace and class as Cameron did. Storm is a guest here, and deserves to be treated with hospitality. Now pull yourself together and snap out of it." For good measure, she put her hands on Belle's shoulders and gave them a shake.

"Okay, well I guess it's no secret where I get my forthright, abrupt nature from," Belle said. She glanced at the wall and saw a painting she had passed several times over the last few days. Previously, she had thought it was an elephant. Now that she was standing so close to it, she could tell it was a moose, or at least it was supposed to be a moose. One antler came out of the top of its head and the other stuck out at a ninety degree angle from the side of its face. Its snout was long, hanging almost to the ground, and it had two bucked teeth hanging out the end of the snout.

Her mother also noticed the painting. "That's cute; one of the kids must have done that when they were little. Lori King is a good mother for hanging that monstrosity in her hallway. That's maternal love for you."

Belle had no reply to that; she was laughing too hard.

When she was finally able to take a breath and wipe her eyes, she followed her mother back to the kitchen. Trying not to draw attention to herself, she slipped in between Cam and Storm. Both of them were eyeing her, trying to figure out if she was all right.

"Everything okay?" Cam finally asked.

"It's fine," Belle said. "I was admiring the painting in the hallway." She darted a glance at Layla who choked on her cornbread.

"That one's my favorite," Josh said with such earnest devotion Belle covered her mouth with her napkin and pretended to cough while Layla dove to the refrigerator, stuck her head in and had her own coughing spell.

For a long time, Storm remained quiet and watchful. He stared at the family as if they were speaking a different language. Probably to him they were as they talked about cows, hunting, fishing, and trucks. Wearing head to toe black and an expensive haircut, he couldn't have stood out more in this sea of flannel, Wranglers, and boots. Belle's father, who had the ability to talk to a stone and get a response, eventually drew him into conversation by astutely asking about his art.

Belle only listened with half an ear until her name came up in the conversation.

"I wouldn't be where I am without Belle. She negotiated with the gallery so they would take a lower commission on my work. And she found a sublet for me so I have more workspace for half the price. She's a miracle worker." He turned to smile at Belle.

"That's our Belle," her father said. "She's always been industrious. When she was ten, she insisted I rearrange my employees' workstations to cut down on the time it took them to scan groceries through their lines. And of course she was right. I know this because she did a productivity study and proved it to me. Each lane shaved an average of twenty percent off their scan time. I didn't have the heart to tell her people came to our store for conversation, and not for convenience."

"With less time spent in line, they had more time to be social," Belle countered.

Storm laughed and patted her leg. "That's my girl."

Cam cleared his throat.

The tension in the room skyrocketed. Storm had no idea why, but he felt the atmospheric shift and lifted his hand from Belle.

"Did Belle tell you we were in school together?" Coy offered.

"No, to be honest, she doesn't talk much about her life before New York. I only knew she was from Montana because I saw her birth certificate when I took her to apply for a passport."

"What did you get a passport for, Belle?" Ivy asked.

Storm answered. "We're planning a trip to London this summer."

Belle winced, hating the way he made it sound. "*I* am planning a trip to London to meet with a publisher." Storm had invited himself along in order to paint. "It's going to be a quick trip, a couple of days."

"London sounds like a nice place for a honeymoon," Cam said.

Belle's mother choked on her iced tea. Her husband pounded her gently on the back.

"No," Storm disagreed. "If you're looking for a good honeymoon destination, you need to go to Paris. I went to school there. It's perfect."

"I'll keep that in mind," Cam said casually. "Though I've always wanted to see Italy, myself."

"Italy's cool," Storm agreed. "Are you engaged?"

"No, but I hope to be soon."

Once again Storm felt the unaccountable tension in the room, and it made him uneasy. There was something he was missing here, something to do with Belle.

"Storm," Belle addressed him for the first time, "where are you staying tonight?"

He shrugged. "I rented a car at the airport. I'll get a hotel room." This proclamation was met with more silence. "What?" he looked around the room and saw everyone staring at him like he had horns and a pitchfork.

"There aren't any hotels in town. The nearest hotel is an hour away," Belle said.

"Oh," Storm said. Not for the first time, he was rethinking what had seemed like a romantic plan to win Belle back.

"You can stay with us," Belle's mother offered generously.

Storm beamed at her. "Thank you. I don't want to put you to any trouble. I wouldn't want to toss Belle out of her room." He turned to give Belle a conspiratorial smile, noting once again the icy silence that had descended over the room. What was with these people? He thought country folk were supposed to be friendly.

"I'm not staying there," Belle said slowly. "I'm staying here." For emphasis she tapped her index finger on the table in front of them.

"Why?" he asked.

She could have told him it was for her work, and it would have been the truth. But she needed to be honest, at least as honest as she could be and still spare his feelings. "We can talk about it later," she said softly. No need to humiliate him in front of the room at large.

Storm didn't think that sounded promising, but maybe she didn't get along with her parents. They seemed nice enough, but he knew from his own experience that looks could be deceiving. He and his own family weren't on the best of terms.

Conversation buzzed around the table. Everyone did their best to try and include Storm, but either jet lag or the unbearable tension was catching up with him because he remained silent, picking sullenly at his food.

At last the meal was over. Belle stood and tapped Storm on the shoulder. "Come with me, please." She turned and left the room with him trailing behind her like a sad puppy. If he had a tail, it would have been tucked between his legs. She led him outside to the porch where they would be guaranteed privacy before turning to face him.

The night was cold. She chafed her arms to warm them. He took a step toward her, arms outstretched, but she held up a hand to ward him off.

"Storm, what are you doing here? We broke up."

He shook his head. "I don't believe that, Belle. This is temporary insanity on your part. I thought if I could come out here, I could make you see that." He sounded uncertain.

"You can't change my mind about this. I like you, I really do. You're a good guy, a nice guy."

He grimaced. "Things never go well when a woman thinks you're nice."

"That's not true. Women worth wanting are looking for a nice guy. But this isn't about that. We're wrong for each other."

"How can you say that? We work great together."

She sighed. She was going to have to be brutal. "No. We don't work together. I work for you. You were right when you said I arrange your life and tell you what to do. I don't think you love me. I think you love what I do for you, but any secretary worth her salary could do the same thing."

"But we've had some good times together."

"We really have. I've had fun with you. I've enjoyed the time we spent together. But I'm not in love with you, and I don't think you're in love with me. I think you're comfortable with me and you don't like to lose, which is a trait I can relate to."

He blew out a breath and studied her. "You're different here. You're softer, gentler. I still think you're having some sort of freak-out about being in the country."

"The country isn't a disease," she said. "It's not something you catch."

"I'm only repeating what I've heard you say, Belle."

"Then I'm a horrible snob," she snapped. She also took a deep breath and blew it out slowly. "I'm sorry. I didn't mean to snap at you.

I don't like hurting you, and I don't want to. But I cannot be in a romantic relationship with you. Please stop pushing."

"You have to push to get what you want, Belle. You taught me that. How many times have I watched you wear someone down to get what you want? Enough to know it's a strategy that works. So you'll have to forgive me for using it on you, but I learned from the best." He settled his hands on her waist and began to urge her closer. Belle placed her palms on his chest, trying to push him away with no success, and that was when the front screen banged open.

"Is this what you want, Belle?" Cam asked calmly.

"No," she replied.

He turned to look at Storm. "Then you'll need to take your hands off her. Now."

Storm looked between them uncertainly. "Belle, what's this about?"

"You'd better hurry up and comply, Storm, because I've seen this scenario played out a lot here. It doesn't end well for you."

He dropped his hands and stumbled back. "What scenario? What are you talking about?"

"She's talking about what happens when someone touches another man's woman. We don't take kindly to that in Montana."

"What are you talking about?" Storm asked, thoroughly confused. "Belle's mine."

Belle put her hands over her face and groaned.

"No, she's not," Cam said in an icy, controlled voice. "I've tried to be polite to you because hospitality demands it, but I won't have you trying to physically force something on Belle she doesn't want."

"What are you talking about?' Storm repeated, dazed and confused.

Oddly, Belle sympathized with him. Nothing in Manhattan had prepared him to interact with a cowboy from Montana. The two men were as different as night and day. To Storm, it was as if Cam was speaking in tongues. But Cam, not understanding how different Storm's world was, thought he was being purposely obtuse. His fuse was almost at an end. If Belle didn't step in now to translate, things would get really ugly.

"Storm, Cam's trying to tell you what I've been trying to spare you. He and I have known each other all our lives. Since I returned home, things have developed between us, and we're together now. He's been waiting on me to tell you, but he's not willing to wait anymore, and he doesn't want you to touch me or mention getting back together again. I'm sorry you had to hear about it like this."

Storm stared at her, disbelief clouding his expression. "It's like *Invasion of the Body Snatchers.* I hear the words coming out of your mouth, but they don't make any sense. Have you joined a cult or something? I mean, who says 'my woman' and goes around threatening someone not to touch her like she's a piece of property? Come on, Belle, it's not the eighteen hundreds."

Previously Belle might have agreed with everything he said. But having spent this time at the ranch seeing close up the special way of life here, she now understood where Cam was coming from.

"I don't think there's a way I could explain it to you in order to make you understand, and I'm sorry if you're hurt and confused. But this," she pointed between herself and Cam, "has nothing to do with us. I would have come to this conclusion without him. You and I don't work. You need to find someone you work with."

"I'm beginning to think you're right. I'm also beginning to think you're insane."

"Hey," Cam took a step toward him. Storm backed up a step and nearly toppled down the stairs.

Belle put a restraining hand on Cam's chest. "He was joking." She turned to Storm. "You can't call women names here in front of their significant others. It's not acceptable behavior, along with threatening or inappropriate touching." This must be what translators at the United Nations felt like, she thought.

"I've got to get out of here," Storm said, sounding panicked. "Tell your parents thanks but no thanks on the room. I'm flying back to sanity as soon as possible." As if to accentuate his point, he stumbled down the steps, scrambled to the rental car, fell into the car, and sped off down the lane.

Cam and Belle stood on the porch, watching him in silence until he was out of sight.

"So that's the type of guy you like," Cam said. He draped his arm on her shoulders. "Should I be concerned he willfully flew back to a city filled with murderers and thugs rather than stay in our idyllic little town with me?"

"It's hard to tell because he was wearing black, but I'm almost positive you made him wet his pants."

They turned to each other and started to laugh. He swept her up in his arms and kissed her. "Come on, woman, let's go tell the others bloodshed has been avoided, thanks to your peacemaking and translation skills."

"Whatever you say, Tarzan."

"You agent, me rancher," he said and, tossing her over his shoulder, carried her inside.

CHAPTER 22

ounder's Day. For once Belle was awake before Layla. She lay blinking up at the ceiling, trying hard not to have an anxiety attack. She was a grownup woman now. She could do this. Nothing bad was going to happen today.

Still, despite her mental pep talk, she remained clutching the blanket to her chest so tightly her knuckles became white and frozen.

Layla woke and, thinking Belle was asleep like usual, paid her no attention as she went about her routine of getting ready. When she left the room, Belle remained frozen in place, unsuccessfully trying to convince herself to let go of the blanket and get up.

The door opened a few minutes later. Cam entered, keeping the door ajar so some light spilled into the room, illuminating the bed. He crawled in beside her fully dressed on top of the blankets, his boots hanging over the edge of the mattress. Gathering her close with both arms, he pressed his face to her neck and inhaled.

"How long have you been awake?" he asked.

"Dunno," she answered, nestling into his embrace. He smelled like leather and horses and she didn't hate it; she didn't hate it at all.

He shifted so he was also lying on his back, also staring at the ceiling. He laced his fingers over his chest. "Nice view up there. I can see why you're not blinking."

She wanted to tell him she didn't think she could do this; she didn't think she could face this day that had brought her so much humiliation in the past. She didn't want to run the risk of, once again, being the girl everyone pointed and laughed at. But of course she didn't. This was still Cameron King, after all, and there was a part of her that refused to show weakness in front of him. Absently she thought that would have to change before they had kids together. She didn't want to have to pretend to be feeling no pain when she was in labor.

That thought startled her, and she jumped, almost upending herself from the bed.

"What?" he asked drowsily.

"I was thinking about having babies. With you."

He propped himself up on his elbow and grinned down at her. "Really?" All trace of sleepiness was gone from his voice. "Tell me more about your plans for me to impregnate you."

She pressed her palm to his cheek and smiled up at him. "Nope."

He captured her free hand and kissed it. "It's really going to be okay today, Belle."

"Is it?" she said absently, not quite believing him.

"Yes. In fact I'm willing to make a wager with you," he said.

She perked up interestedly. "What?"

"I bet you will have fun today."

"What are you willing to bet?" she asked.

He searched his mind, trying to find something he could offer that she would want. A new horse or tractor wouldn't cut it here. "I bet you naming rights to our first child."

Belle's heart turned over before lurching up to lodge in her throat. This was too much, too soon. They hadn't worked out the tricky problem of having several states between them, let alone begun to talk marriage or children. Plus if they ever did get married or have children, she wanted to choose their names together.

Then she remembered some of the names Cam had mentioned he

liked, along with the fact that he seemed to think his mother's artwork should be in the Louvre, and she began to see the potential in the bet. The man had more heart than sense sometimes.

"Okay, but I get to choose the middle name, too. Don't try to weasel in a BillyJohn or JimmyJoeDohickey."

"Deal." He held up his hand as if taking an oath. "I swear if you don't have fun today you will retain sole naming rights to our first-born child, both first and middle names. Now it's your turn." He nudged her with his boot.

"I," she started, but he stopped her.

"Put up your hand and make it official."

"Where does it say sticking your hand in the air makes things official?" she groused, but she complied, raising her hand in the air. "I swear if I have fun today I will relinquish all rights to naming our first child, including first and middle name."

"Good," he said. "Now raise your other hand the same way."

She raised her other hand, not sure what he was doing until he took both her hands in his, lacing their fingers together, then he leaned over her, pressing her into the mattress. "Now kiss me."

"I have morning breath," she said, trying not to move her lips.

"I'll have to get used to it at some point. Might as well be now," he said. Then, denying her any further protest, he kissed her.

* * *

A COUPLE OF HOURS LATER, they were on their way. The family was so large they had to take several trucks.

"If you bought a conversion van, you wouldn't have to have so many trucks. Then everyone could fit in one car," Belle said over breakfast. When she looked up at the men's silent faces, she was almost certain she could hear crickets chirping. The only sound that shattered the silence was Ivy's giggle, which she tried to cover with her hand.

"Have you ever seen a rancher driving a conversion van?" Cam asked at last. "No. It's because no one wants to look like a traveling family band." That comment was met with laughter and high fives from his brothers.

"Yes, it's much less ridiculous to show up in four separate trucks like stragglers from a Willie Nelson concert," Belle said. She held up her hand to Ivy and Layla who high fived her.

"Until Josh gets married, you ladies are outnumbered, and we'll keep our trucks," Coy said.

"And any woman who wants to be with me will have to like trucks," Josh added.

Cam laughed. "Keep making a list, buddy. It worked out well for me." He winked at Belle.

"I don't see what the big deal is," Josh said. "You find what you want in a girl, and you fall in love. End of story."

"Josh King, the Shakespeare of Montana," Cade said.

"If it's so easy, why haven't you done it yet?" Coy asked. To the family's knowledge, Josh had never had a girlfriend.

"I'm biding my time," Josh said in his usual serious tone. "And when it happens, it's going to be epic. And you'll all feel bad for making fun of me."

"You don't understand much about brotherly love if you think we'll ever feel bad about making fun of you," Coy said.

"Okay, stop picking on Josh," Ivy said. "Let him hold on to his ideals as long as possible."

"You always take his side," Coy pouted.

"Because I know what it's like to be the youngest," Ivy said. "I have five older brothers," she explained to Belle.

Cade shuddered. "Let's not talk about them. I always have the feeling if we mention them they'll somehow show up. I don't think the town has recovered from their last visit."

"We'd better get going," Cam announced. "I'm anxious to get the festivities started. Little Sunshine JimJoeDohickey and I have a lot riding on this day."

"Who?" Layla asked.

"I'm trying out names to see how they feel."

Belle groaned and dropped her head to the table. "What have I done?"

Cam stood and helped her carry her bag to his truck. "What's in this thing? You know Founder's Day is only one day, right?"

"I packed a couple of changes of clothes, a first aid kit, extra shoes, a dress for the dance tonight, and the number of a good therapist in Manhattan in case I need it at some point during the day," Belle replied.

Cam helped her into the truck and leaned over to kiss her cheek. "Life was really boring without you, Belle."

"Right now boring sounds great. Boring doesn't end in trips to the emergency room, or news footage that lingers on the internet for generations, or the taste of blood sadly reminding me of my first kiss. Boring is what I want for today."

"Sorry to disappoint you, but today is not going to be boring. Little Corncob BillyJo is depending on me to show you a good time."

"Corncob? Really?"

"It's a family name. I had an uncle Corncob." He glanced at her. "What, no comment?"

"No, because I'm not sure if you're kidding. But please know deep inside my heart, a part of me has died."

He smirked at her. "See, you're already having fun."

She shook her head. "It doesn't count until we're officially at Founder's Day. And then, if past history is any indication, I'll probably immediately get swept up in a twister or stuck in a hay baler and your little bet will go up in flames. Most likely along with my hair because, statistically speaking, I'm due to catch on fire at one of these events."

He laughed so hard he got a stitch in his side and had to press his hand to his abdomen. "Well at least *I'm* going to have fun today."

"I'm pretty sure that's the point of Founder's Day, for Belle Landry to provide entertainment for everyone else." She crossed her arms over her chest, stared out her window, and remained silent the rest of the way to town.

CHAPTER 23

They arrived at the festival. Cam found parking near his brothers and turned off the truck, but Belle made no move to leave the vehicle. He went over to her side and opened the door, but she remained staring resolutely through the front windshield.

"Isabelle," he called softly. "Come here, girl." He patted his leg a few times and made kissing noises at her.

She turned to scowl at him. "I am not a cat at the vet's office." She scooted to the edge of the seat and hopped down, refusing his help.

Undaunted by her bad temper, he looped his arm over her shoulders and led her in the direction of Main Street. Her eyes swept the landscape furtively, as if looking for an attack she knew to be imminent.

"Try to relax, Sweet," he said soothingly. "I'm not going to leave you today."

Those were the magic words to ease the tense set of her shoulders. Whatever happened today, Cam would be with her. Then she tensed as a new thought occurred to her.

"I don't want to be the one responsible for your death."

"Oh, Belle," he said, rolling his eyes.

A large crowd, probably everyone in town, was gathered around the stage at the public square in the center of town. Every year the day began here with a short speech by the mayor, the national anthem, and a prayer by one of the local citizens. Belle and Cam arrived as the mayor was finishing his welcoming speech and then a little girl stood to sing the national anthem.

Belle felt slightly evil for wishing the kid would mess up and pass out as she had done all those years ago, but no such luck. The girl performed perfectly, even hitting all the high notes on key. "Show off," Belle muttered. Beside her Cam pinched her waist.

This year, Cade had been chosen to give the opening prayer. A makeshift ramp had been built ascending to the platform. The crowd remained silent while Layla helped wheel him to the top. She turned to go when they reached the stage, but he grasped her wrist to hold her back.

"My girlfriend thinks I'm here to give the prayer," he said.

Belle looked at Cam in surprise. She had thought the same thing. Cam didn't return her look, though. He remained staring placidly at the stage.

"The truth is that for the last two years, I've already been praying, hoping by some miracle I would be able to get down on one knee and do things the proper way. But even though I've realized that's never going to happen, I can't help feeling like Layla, awesome and amazing as she is, deserves to have everything done the right way. So I'm going to do it by proxy."

As if by some prearranged agreement, every man in attendance knelt on one knee, holding their clasped hands upraised toward Layla who stood on the stage in shock, her hands over her mouth and tears streaming down her face. Belle tore her eyes off Layla to look around at the crowd, noting the three remaining King boys kneeling and smiling, and a two year old boy down on one knee, his hands clasped at his chest. And then there was old Mr. Carter who was ninety if he was a day, kneeling with his cane propped beside him. Her attention returned to the stage as Cade began speaking again.

"Layla, you came into my life when I needed you most, helping me through the most difficult time I'll probably ever experience. You made our house a home again, and I can't imagine spending a day without you. Will you finally make it official and be my wife?"

Layla nodded, too choked up to speak.

Cade reached for her hand and slipped a ring on her finger before turning to the smiling audience. "She said yes. I guess you can stand up now."

Chuckles and applause broke out all around while Layla leaned down and kissed Cade.

"Does everyone who knelt get one of those?" a young cowboy asked, causing the crowd to laugh again.

"No," Cade said emphatically.

Cam quirked an eyebrow at Belle. "Having fun yet?"

She swiped impatiently at her eyes. "Technically being incredibly touched and humbled does not count as having fun so, no."

"That's okay," Cam said. "The day's only getting started."

Next he led her to the baseball field where every year the alumni baseball players competed against the current high school team. Last time she was here, she had watched as one of the high school kids. It felt strange to be on the other side of the fence, even though twenty-two wasn't old by any stretch of the imagination.

Josh was on the current baseball team and ran out to join his teammates. The three remaining brothers had all played, but of course Cade wouldn't be joining Coy and Cam on the field today. He didn't seem to mind staying behind, however. He and Layla were still basking in the glow of his proposal. They sat cuddled up together in Cade's chair while Belle and Ivy sat beside them on the uncomfortable bench.

Belle had never been a sports enthusiast and today was no different. She watched half-heartedly while scanning the crowd, picking out familiar faces.

"Cam's coming up to bat," Ivy told her.

That worked to snap her attention back to the field. Cam selected his bat, strode toward the plate, and then turned to look back at Belle. He pointed to the outfield and said, loudly, "This one is for you, Belle."

Belle felt her face flame. "Oh, sweet mercy, he's lost his mind," she muttered. All around the crowd, people smiled and nudged each other with their elbows, probably at having the rumor of Belle and Cam's relationship confirmed.

Even though she was slightly mortified at being the center of attention, there was an immature, girly part of her that was secretly thrilled at the action. It was a tradition in the town for the high school boys to signal to their girlfriends, dedicating their impending home-runs to them.

As a teenager, Belle had watched the ritual with a mixture of envy and revulsion. Certainly no one had ever dedicated a hit to her before. And, if she were being honest, part of her gratification today came from the fact that people were no doubt impressed by the match she had made with Cam. The Kings were the closest thing the town had to royalty. Their family had lived there for generations. Their ranch was large and prosperous. The four brothers were well known and liked in the community. Cam, even though he was a twin, was regarded as the oldest and therefore the head of the clan. Despite his reputation as a too-serious workaholic, he was a much-desired commodity by the available women of the community. And he had chosen her, nerdy Isabelle Landry who had always been a misfit.

"Dreamy sigh," she said, causing Ivy to giggle. "I have really got to stop speaking every thought out loud."

"Please don't," Ivy said. "I haven't laughed this much since my brothers' last visit."

The alumni won the game by one run, which Cam stubbornly insisted was the run he had dedicated to Belle, and then it was time for the parade. They wove their way through the crowd slowly because they were stopped every few feet by people wanting to say hello and talk about the weather, cows, the economy, and anything else they could think of. Seemingly everyone remembered Belle, but not one person asked her about New York or referred to the fact that she had been away for the last four years.

"It's like I never left," she commented irritably to Cam.

"You're a part of us," he said. "People view your time in New York as a temporary aberration. They probably think you've come back to stay, having decided the debauchery of the big city was too much."

She stopped short. "But that's not how it is."

"I know," he said patiently, urging her forward again. "I didn't say that's the way it is; I said that's what people believe. And, really, does it matter what anyone else thinks?"

"No," she said, but she didn't believe her words. It shouldn't have mattered all those years ago that she was an outcast here, like it shouldn't matter that people should have noticed her triumphant return. But it did. She wanted atonement for the pain this town had caused her growing up, and she wanted recognition for the achievements she had accomplished since leaving.

But Cam was right; wanting those things was petty. Did she really expect people to remember every time they laughed at or excluded her? Did she want to wear a sandwich board listing her salary and professional affiliations? When it came down to it, she couldn't have it both ways. She couldn't make people recognize the changes in her without forcing them to remember her as she had been.

"Belle," Cam said patiently, "in some ways our community is like our family. You love and accept them no matter what. There are always going to be things that make you angry, but if you don't accept faults, forgive wounds, and move on then you're consciously removing yourself from the family. Out here where there are so few of us and conditions are harsh, community isn't important—it's essential. Yes, they gossip too much and are occasionally ignorant or mean-spirited, but they're a part of us. They've made us who we are almost as much as our parents have." He pulled her to a stop beside him and looked down at her. "Like it or not, you're a part of us, and we're a part of you. You can go to New York and try to look fancy and sophisticated but inside you'll always be Isabelle Landry from the middle-of-nowhere Montana. And from where I'm standing, that's a very good thing."

Her lips quavered and her eyes watered as she looked up at him. "Saying sweet things that make me cry is definitely not my definition of fun," she said, sniffling.

"Then how's this for fun?" He wheeled her around so she could see where they were standing. Behind them was the senior center where she had run the float tractor off the road, plowing into the crowd. "Look," Cam whispered, pointing to a spot about ten feet away.

There sat Mr. Whethers, the man who'd had the heart attack when he saw the tractor barreling toward him. And in his hands was an open bag of pork rinds.

"See? He's fine," Cam said. "Never let it be said that Belle Landry is a murderer."

"Belle Landry?" the old woman beside them looked up in alarm from her folding chair.

"Yes, ma'am, this is Belle Landry," Cam said.

The woman gave a yelp of alarm and stood to her feet as quickly as her shaky knees would allow. "Out of my way," she hollered. Reaching for her walker, she began shuffling toward the safety of the senior center at a furious pace, using the wheels of the walker to shove people out of her path.

"Okay, that didn't go like I planned," Cam said, staring at the spot the frightened old woman had vacated. Beside him, Belle was making little hiccupping sounds. Thinking he had destroyed whatever was left of her self-esteem, he gently cupped her chin and tipped her face up. "Belle it's okay, she…" He cut off when he realized she wasn't crying; she was laughing. Actually, she *was* crying, but it was from laughing so hard.

"That was the funniest thing I have ever seen," Belle said, ineffectively swiping at her tears. "Did you see how fast she was moving to get away from me? I'm tempted to circulate around the crowd of old people and say 'boo' a few times to see what happens."

"Let's not push our luck. A second heart attack might be the end of Mr. Whethers."

Belle doubled over, howling with laughter. Around them people turned to look and smiled, thinking it was good to see Cameron King smiling for a change. He was far too stuffy to suit most people in the community.

When the parade ended, Cam and Belle strolled hand in hand through the booths and displays that lined the side streets.

"There it is," Cam said reverentially when they reached the dunking booth. "Maybe I should buy it and have it bronzed."

Belle elbowed him in the stomach.

"I'm serious," Cam continued. "Now that I look back on it, I'm fairly certain that was the day I fell in love with you."

"The day you didn't once look at my face so you had no idea it was me you were ogling?"

"Yes, that day," he said, staring unblinkingly at the tank. "The best day ever."

"Ugh, men," Belle huffed and jerked away from him.

He caught up with her, grasped her hand, and led her behind the booth to a spot where three booths converged, creating a small, private hideaway. "Is this the spot?" he asked.

She sighed. "Yes, this is where I had my nightmare of a first kiss."

He turned her to face him and gently cupped her face in his hands. "Sometimes I think the only way to erase a bad memory is to replace it with a good one. Belle, if I could turn back the clock to when we were fourteen, I would give anything to be the guy who kissed you first, even if I had to have a hundred stitches because of it. I love you." He bent and kissed her. It wasn't a passionate kiss. It was gentle, his lips barely applying pressure to hers. And it was perfect.

CHAPTER 24

*B*elle was hungry, but there was one more place Cam wanted to see at the festival. They compromised by picking up food they could carry with them and ate while walking.

"I've never been to the coon trials," Belle said. Hunting was a big event in the area. Tourists came for big game hunting, but the locals preferred to stick to smaller prey. For that reason, raccoon hunting was a favorite hobby of many. And no one hunted raccoons without hound dogs. Therefore, every Founder's Day, the town held its annual coon dog competition, sort of a triathlon for hunting dogs.

Belle had never gone for two reasons. The first was that she couldn't care less about hunting and had always thought it was sort of sad the poor raccoons were scared out of their wits for the sake of competition. The second was that the competition was held on the other side of town and she had always been too lazy to walk there.

But now the walk provided the perfect opportunity for Belle and Cam to finish their food and wipe their fingers on their napkins before they arrived at the contest. They arrived in time for the water portion of the trials. At the start of the competition, the dogs were given the scent of the raccoons and told to track them. Then they were led through an obstacle course where the raccoons had previously been released. Of course they didn't find the raccoons there; that would have been too easy. Instead, the raccoons were boxed up and hauled to the middle of the small lake in the center of the park. They waited nervously on pedestals in their boxes, surrounded by water, until the dogs eventually caught the scent and swam out to "tree" their prey. The first dog to reach a raccoon was the winner.

"I think it's mean," Belle said to Cam. She whispered because she knew her opinion wasn't a popular one.

"They let the raccoons go when they're done. True, they're probably frightened out of their wits, but they're not injured."

"That's something, I guess." She looked around, trying to garner an ounce of enthusiasm for the event. The most she could say was that she thought the dogs were cute with their giant floppy ears, and she laughed at the sounds they made as they bayed excitedly.

Finally, the dogs nosed toward the edge of the water, realizing at last their prey was in the pond. The first dog fearlessly dove in, paddling furiously toward a raccoon in the center.

At this point, Belle became interested. She leaned forward, breathless to see which dog would be the first to reach a raccoon. And that was when it happened. The crowd behind her jostled forward too, knocking her off balance. Cam's arms windmilled as he grasped for her, but it was too late; she was in the lake. Not only that, but her presence diverted the dogs from their goal. Instead of swimming toward the raccoons, they changed course, swimming for her as fast as they could and baying wildly.

The dogs reached her almost simultaneously. She felt a moment of panic they might mistake her for a raccoon, but quickly realized there was no need for fear. The dogs were friendly. Too friendly. As if on cue, all of them began eagerly licking any part of her they could reach while the crowd above howled with laughter.

She tried extricating herself from the dogs as she swam to the ladder at the edge of the pier, but the dogs came with her as if they were some sort of bon voyage committee, bound to see her through her time in the water.

Cam was waiting at the top of the ladder. He put an arm down and hauled her up.

"I'll go get your bag from the truck. You can shower at your parents' house." With that, he put his arm around her and led her down the street, waving away anyone who tried to talk to them.

They walked in silence to the house where she grew up. Cam left her at the door without a word and sprinted away to gather her things. She let herself in with the key under the mat and went down the hall to the bathroom. Her contacts were water logged, so she took them out and put them in a spare case she always kept in the drawer. She was blind without them, but she didn't have her glasses on her. Her old glasses from high school were in the drawer. She fished them out, put them on, and looked at herself in the mirror.

She was dripping wet with stinky lake water. Her clothes were stained from the rust in the water and would probably never come clean again. Her hair was wet and turning frizzy where it started to dry. Her makeup was long gone. She wore the same glasses she had worn during all four years of high school. And she had fallen in a lake in front of half of the town. On Founder's Day.

But, oddly, she couldn't seem to feel anything other than amusement. True, she looked the same as she had when she had been here four years ago. And also true that, yet again, something terribly embarrassing had happened to her on this wretched day. But something had changed. *She* had changed. No longer was she an insecure kid, unsure of her place in the world. She was a successful professional living in Manhattan. She wasn't alone anymore; she had Cam, and his family, and her family, and even this town. Despite the fact that she might take some ribbing over her time in the water today, she knew it would be light-hearted fun and not mean-spirited mockery.

But of course Cam wasn't privy to these new thoughts in her head. He was certain the day was ruined, and so was her psyche. For that reason, when he knocked on the door of the bathroom he was shocked when a laughing Belle opened the door and threw herself into his arms.

"I fell in the lake and was licked by a pack of dogs," she said between laughter.

He was too startled to laugh with her. "Uh, okay," he said warily. Was she having some sort of mental break?

"Really, when you think about it, this isn't a setback for me. It's a victory for raccoons everywhere." She took the bag from him and shut the door, locking it for good measure before her words finally sank in, and then Cam began to laugh. When she stepped out of the shower and poked her head out the door, he was lying on the floor, doubled over with laughter.

* * *

THERE WAS one final event left of the evening, and it was the one Belle had been looking forward to all day. When she emerged re-put together after her lake bath, Cam had finally stopped laughing. Instead he gawked at her in a flattering way that set her heart thrumming.

"You look beautiful, my Belle," he said softly.

"Thank you," she said, glancing down self-consciously. "I had to borrow a dress from Ivy because I only brought the one. It didn't seem appropriate for a Founder's Day dance."

"This is perfect," Cam said as he took in her soft, pastel dress. "You look like a country girl for the first time since you came home."

Coming from him, that was high praise, and she tried to take it for the compliment it was.

"Ready?" he asked. He held out his hand to her.

"Yes," she said, placing her hand in his and allowing him to lead her outside. The sun was starting to set and the air smelled faintly of fall, even though it had been known to snow as early as September here. They walked in silence, hand in hand to the dance already in progress at the public square. She saw Cade and Layla, sitting off to the side in the shadows. Layla was still sitting in his lap and they were talking low and soft together, touching each other's faces as they traded smiles. She wondered if they had changed positions all day.

Coy and Ivy were on the dance floor, swaying gently, gazing into each other's eyes and looking very much like the newlyweds they were. Belle searched until she saw Josh off to the side talking to a group of cowboys and trying to pretend he didn't notice the group of girls to his right. One blond in particular was darting him plenty of glances under her lashes.

Cam took her hand and led her onto the raised platform that made up the dance floor. He tucked her hand against his chest and led her in a slow dance.

"Cam, at what point are we going to address the elephant in the room?" she asked. "I'm flying to New York tomorrow."

"So am I," he reminded her.

"Yes, but," she started, but he put his finger to her lips to halt her.

"Not now, Belle. Please."

"Okay," she said. She pushed all unsettling thoughts from her mind and concentrated on the sheer joy of being in his arms and swaying gently to the music. After a while, they took a break to get a drink from the concession stand. Cam left her to retrieve their drinks and a girl walked up to her, dangling a toddler with one hand and carrying an infant in her other arm. As the woman drew closer, Belle was filled with both recognition and dread. It was Marissa, the girl she had thrown up on when she confessed her love to Coy, the girl who had laughed at her.

"Belle Landry," Marissa declared. "I heard you were back in town."

"Hello, Marissa," Belle said. "Are both these yours?" She pointed to the children, hoping Marissa wouldn't try to make her touch one.

"Yes, they're mine, and Pete's hinting he's ready for another. I told him that would be great, but he has to carry and deliver it this time." She shifted the baby to her other arm and let go of the toddler who instantly darted away. "Listen, Belle, I know this is out of the blue, and you probably don't even remember, but I wanted to apologize to you about something."

Belle froze. *Please don't bring up that day, please, please, please.*

"It actually happened on Founder's Day when we were seniors. I was laughing at you, and I didn't realize how sick you were until you threw up. It's just, you were speaking gibberish. I thought you were purposely trying to be funny. I've felt so bad I laughed at someone who was already sick."

"I was speaking gibberish?" Belle asked.

Marissa nodded. "You came up to me and Coy, flapping your arms and making noises, mostly 'b-b-b-b.' I thought you were playing a joke on us, but Coy had the foresight to know you were sick. I'm sorry."

"So, not to beat a dead horse, but I didn't say any understandable words that day?"

"None I remember, unless it was some language I don't under-stand." She giggled. "Sorry. This is horrible. I'm supposed to be apologizing, and I'm still laughing over it. Really mature, Marissa."

"No, please don't apologize," Belle said. "I feel horrible I threw up on you." She tried to sound contrite, but she, too, started to giggle. By the time Cam reached them with their drinks, the two women were leaning against a pole laughing and talking like old friends.

After that, Cam and Belle returned to the dance floor. Like before when they went to the charity function in the city, they danced every dance together. When the caller announced it was the last dance, Cam snuggled her closer and looked deeply into her eyes.

"Be honest. Did you have fun today?"

She paused, considering, and then she rested her head on his chest in defeat. "Let's say I'll get busy searching for monogrammed layettes for little Sunshine Corncob BillyBob JoJim."

"To be clear, you're saying I won, right?" he asked.

She pulled away slightly to look up at him. "I'm saying today I had what was possibly the most fun ever, and I love you very much for making it possible."

"Can't bring yourself to say the words 'You won,' huh, Belle?"

"Never in a million years," she said.

"That's my Belle," he said. "Now lets go home."

* * *

THEIR FLIGHT WASN'T until the next evening. Belle spent the morning packing and trying not to think of what lay before them.

In the kitchen, Layla was busy arranging to make her first batch of caramels to ship to the buyer. Belle's mother had come to help her get organized and the two women were chattering excitedly. Because it was Saturday, and because Belle was leaving, Cade and Coy took some time off their duties to see her off. Josh was busy with his friends, but he had said goodbye that morning, awkwardly hugging her and ducking his head when she kissed his cheek.

Ivy was in the barn checking her horses, but she would be returning before the big departure, too. Except for her father who was at his store, Belle realized everyone she cared about in Montana was right there, and she got a little choked up at the sight of everyone together, talking and laughing. She had no idea when she would see them again, and she already missed them.

But there was a part of her that missed New York, too. She missed the owner of the company who had become like a surrogate father to her. She missed her boss, Nancy, who was the busiest person Belle had ever met. She missed her small group of artsy friends. No doubt Storm had circulated the story of their breakup by now, and Belle wondered how she would be received when she returned. She missed her doorman, Larry, who told her a corny joke every morning, and she even missed the hot dog vendor who sold her lunch most days of the week.

How was it possible to want to be in two places at the same time? Instead of being torn between two men, she was torn between two locations. She wanted them both, but could only choose one. Cam was here, and that was a big factor in Montana's favor, but her career was in New York. She had worked too hard to give it up now.

"Ready?" Cam asked, startling her out of her mental debate.

"As I'll ever be," she said, her voice quavering slightly. He squeezed her shoulder and turned to say goodbye to his family. He would only be gone a few days, so there was no heartfelt, prolonged goodbye for him.

But for Belle, she had no idea when she might return. She hugged and kissed everyone twice and then invited them all to New York. They vaguely promised to visit, but they all knew they never would. There was too much to be done on the ranch, and New York was too big and too far away.

"It really is something to see," her mother added helpfully with a pat of Belle's cheek.

"Thanks, Mom," she said, hugging her mother one more time. "I'll try to get home again soon."

"Do your best, baby," her mother said, smoothing down her hair and kissing her forehead.

Belle nodded, too choked up to reply. Coy and Cam carried her bags to the car, leaving her nothing to do but wave goodbye, which she did furiously as if a few flutters of her hand could convey all she was feeling.

"You okay?" Cam asked. He rested his hand on her knee and gave it a light squeeze.

She nodded, not sure she meant it.

"Have you decided what you're going to do with me in New York?" he asked.

She nodded again, trying to regain her voice. "I've got a plan."

"Why does that not surprise me?" he said.

"I just want you to like it," she said.

"What you love, I'll love, Belle. Or at least I'll respect that you love it."

"I know," she said, and she did know. Pickup trucks, rifles, and fishing poles weren't her thing, but they were his and for that reason she could respect them.

During the long drive to the airport and then their flight, they made meaningless small talk about whatever came to mind. There were too many big things that needed to be talked about, so of course they didn't, focusing instead on whether country music was superior to jazz, or vice versa. Secretly, Belle had always liked country music and it was strangely popular in New York City, but she didn't tell

Cam, preferring instead to let him find out for himself and be surprised.

When they touched down in New York, Belle took over. She easily navigated them through JFK and then hailed a taxi. It would cost a fortune to take a cab into Manhattan from the airport, but she hadn't thought to schedule a car service, and there was no way she was dragging all her suitcases on the subway. Plus, because of the time difference, it was very late in New York by the time they arrived. She directed the driver to the hotel she had booked for Cam and sat back, closing her eyes.

"I'm not staying with you?" Cam asked.

"I only have one bedroom," she explained, telling him more than he'd asked. "And my apartment is tiny."

"Interesting," he said.

"What," she said absently, feeling suddenly sleepy.

"That Montana values die hard," he said.

She opened her eyes and looked out the window, not responding. He took her hand and squeezed. "I like that about you, Belle."

"Good," she said, tracing her finger on the windowpane.

They reached his hotel and she asked the cabbie to wait while she checked him in. "The agency is paying for your stay," she explained to Cam as he took in the luxury of the hotel lobby.

"The agency has good taste," he said.

She made the proper arrangements at the desk and walked a few feet away to say goodbye to Cam.

"Stay with me," he begged.

She was taken aback by the request after their conversation in the car.

"That's not what I meant," he said. "You said it's a suite. I'll sleep on the couch. I can't stand the thought of you going home alone this late at night."

She smiled and pressed her palm to his cheek. "Cam, I do it all the time."

"Not when I'm here. Please. I won't sleep a wink if I have to worry about you all night."

"Okay," she capitulated, partly because she was exhausted and the thought of driving across town to her apartment was more than she could handle right now. They went outside and Cam retrieved their bags while she paid the cabbie. The doorman carried their bags to the room and she tipped him, too.

"Doesn't anyone do anything out of the kindness of his heart here?" Cam asked.

"Sure, but five bucks goes a long way toward keeping the kindness flowing," she told him. "If in doubt, tip it out."

"You made that up, didn't you?"

She grinned at him. "I thought it was pretty good for someone who's sleep deprived and has no talent for writing."

He laughed. "So it was. I am officially kissing you goodnight, sleepy girl." He kissed her and walked into the small sitting area, closing the door behind him. He dawdled, pressing his palm to the door. Sensing his hesitation, she locked it, smiling when she heard him laugh and mutter, "Good call."

After quickly washing off her makeup and brushing her teeth, she crawled between the sheets and fell asleep.

The next morning she waited until she had showered and changed before unlocking the door to the sitting room. No need to disappoint him with the "before" version of herself when it was so easy to put herself together. Cam sat on the couch, reading a paper and grinning at her when she opened the door.

"You don't trust me at all, do you?"

"No," she answered bluntly.

"Smart girl," he said. He set aside the paper and reached for her, pulling her into his lap before burying his face in her hair and inhaling. "You smell nice."

"Thank you. How long have you been awake?"

"I'm programmed to wake up at four Montana time, so I guess that would be six here."

"Aw, you're going to be too tired to enjoy the city today."

"I won't. I'm used to functioning on not much sleep. But I have to warn you I'll probably stay on Montana time, and that means I'll most likely conk out at around eight or so."

"That's okay," she assured him. "It means we need to get started as soon as possible. Are you ready?"

He looked down as she did, realizing he was wearing pajama pants and no shirt. "Not unless the dress code is radically different here."

She trailed a finger over his chest. "I'm going to miss those Montana ticks."

"I'm beginning to worry about you and the ticks," he said.

"You should be worried you're so slow to catch on to my devious plots to get your shirt off," she told him.

His jaw dropped. "And you, pretending to be so innocent."

"I'm not pretending. Now go get ready." She slid off his lap and shooed him toward the direction of the door. "We have lots to do today, not the least of which is to legally make me your agent."

"All right," he grumbled. He grabbed his bag and headed toward the bathroom. A few minutes later, she heard the shower running and Cam's voice belting out a country tune. Smiling, she picked up the phone and called her office.

Two hours later, she was leading him toward her office in the huge skyscraper her company called home. They had lingered over a leisurely breakfast at her favorite restaurant. Today it hadn't disappointed with its warm croissants and fresh-squeezed juice. Of course Cam had ordered a heartier meal, but he thoroughly enjoyed his food, declaring it the best bacon he had ever eaten.

"I can't believe you work on the fiftieth floor," he said as she led him through the maze of cubicles to her office.

"There's my office," she pointed.

"You have a door. That must mean you're important."

"You catch on quick," she told him. Her secretary had left the necessary paperwork lying on her desk. She slid it toward Cam and motioned for him to have a seat in one of the leather chairs across from her desk. While he read his contract, she attempted to catch up on a few emails.

"I'm ready," he said. "Can I borrow a pen?"

She pulled a pen out of her desk and slid it to him. He signed and held the pen out to her. "Your turn." She stood and came around to stand beside him, leaning over to sign beneath his name. He slid his hand up to rest on the back of her thigh, just under her skirt, and that was when her boss, Nancy, poked her head into the room.

"Oh," Nancy said. "Hello. You must be Belle's new author."

"Yes, ma'am." Cam stood, whipped off his hat, and held out his hand to Nancy. She beamed at him before turning her attention to Belle.

She had been nervous when Belle informed her that her new writer was a cowboy with no previous experience, and then she had grown downright worried when she learned the two were old friends from high school. Those situations usually didn't work out well. But then Belle sent her a copy of the book. Despite Nancy's busy schedule, she hadn't been able to put the book down, staying up until four in the morning to finish it. And now, seeing there was more than friendship between the two, her elation grew almost to delirium. Cameron King was going to be huge, and he was going to make them a boatload of money. Seeing the obvious love for Belle in his eyes made her feel secure they would never lose his business.

"Mr. King, I have to tell you I loved your book. Belle was right; you're going to be a hit. I wouldn't be surprised if there's a bidding war."

"Please call me Cam. And with Belle on the job, I'm fairly certain there will be," Cam said.

"That's true," Nancy said. "Well, I'll leave you two alone. Have a pleasant visit, Cam, and if you need anything at all, please let us know."

They exchanged another handshake and Nancy let herself out of the office.

"Does everyone work on Saturdays?" Cam asked.

"No, not the secretaries."

"That seems sort of backwards," Cam said. "The bosses working weekends and the underlings being off."

Belle giggled. "I'll make sure and tell my secretary he's an underling. He'll like that."

Cam frowned. "Why does your secretary have to be a man?"

"Because he was born that way," she said.

He crossed his arms over his chest.

"This is New York. Leave your Montana jealousy behind," she said.

"My jealousy isn't dependent on geography," he said. "But I'll let it go because I trust you and because, after meeting your boyfriend, I'm not very threatened by the men of Manhattan."

"Good. Let's go."

"Where are we going?"

"We're taking a tour so you can see all the touristy stuff, and then I'll show you some off the beaten path stuff when that's done."

The tour hit all the major highlights, including a view of the Statue of Liberty, the Empire State Building, Rockefeller Center, and Central Park. As she knew he would, Cam loved Central Park and was amazed there was such a beautiful green space in the middle of the city. But to her further surprise, he seemed to enjoy everything she showed him, taking pictures to show the family when he returned back home.

That night for supper, she took him to Peter Luger steakhouse in Brooklyn. Besides being the premiere steakhouse in the country, it was family owned. She called in a few favors and arranged a tour of the meat locker for after their meal. Cam was properly impressed not only with the food, but with the knowledge of the meat buyer who personally gave him a tour. The meat buyer was equally enthralled when she learned he was a cattle rancher and the two spent a long time talking business. By the end of the evening, she arranged a visit to Montana to check out his operation.

"This has been a great day, Belle," Cam said on the cab ride to her apartment. He hadn't been there yet, and she was nervous about his reaction.

"I'm glad you had fun," she said. "It's important to me you like it here."

"I told you I would."

"Yes, but you said you would like it because I like it. I want you to like it because it appeals to you," she said.

"Why? Do you think I plan to live here?" he asked.

"No, of course not. But I hope you'll visit sometime."

"Is that what you want to happen between us, Belle? Occasional visits?"

"Of course not, Cam. But I don't see any other solution."

The cab reached her apartment complex and pulled over. Belle, glad for the distraction, pulled out the money and paid before turning to lead Cam up to her apartment.

"Ms. Landry," the nighttime doorman tipped his hat politely and gave Cam a curious stare. Belle bit back a smile. All day long, heads had been turning to look at the tall cowboy with the white Stetson and leather boots, but Cam paid the looks no attention, seemingly as comfortable here as he was on his ranch in Montana.

It was a short, tense, and silent elevator ride up to her apartment. "Here we are," she said unnecessarily as she stopped and pulled out her key. Cam took it from her and opened the door when they both realized her hands were shaking. She had no idea what was about to happen between them, but she knew it was going to be monumental, with the ability to make or break them.

"This is it," she said. She waved her hand and encompassed the entire apartment, except for her tiny bedroom, hidden behind a door.

"It's cute," he said.

"It's smaller than Layla's bedroom at the ranch, but, believe it or not, this is a major step up for me."

"No, really, it's nice. I'm not totally ignorant about real estate in Manhattan. I know this is a nice apartment."

His kindness reassured her and she took a deep breath before leading him to the couch. They sat and faced each other.

"So what's your miraculous solution to our problem?" she prodded.

"You can't leave New York," he said.

She shook her head.

"And I can't leave Montana," he continued.

She shook her head again.

"So I think we should meet in the middle."

"Ohio?" she guessed.

"You're thinking too literally, Belle. I mean I'll move to New York if you'll move to Montana. We'll split our time living half the year in each place."

Her jaw dropped before she quickly recovered. "But New York is the epicenter of the publishing industry."

"And a job doesn't get more dependent on a location than ranching. It's not like I can load the cows in a plane with me. But I'm willing to arrange what I need to in order to make this work. Are you?"

She thought about it for one breathless moment while he stared at her with his heart in his eyes. "Yes. I'll make it work." It wouldn't be easy, and it would take some convincing, but she had proved she could work long distance, at least part of the year. And she had just signed a new, potentially huge client. "If you keep writing impending bestsellers, it would give me a lot more leverage to negotiate my location," she added.

"I'll do my best," he said. He leaned forward and kissed her, and then broke off to yawn. "Sorry."

"Want to have a cup of coffee before you head back to your hotel?"

"That sounds nice," he said.

"I'll be right back." She stood, scurried into the postage stamp kitchen and brewed a pot of decaf for them. When she exited with a loaded tray, Cam was fast asleep, slumped over on her couch. She thought about waking him, then decided against it. She didn't want to be away from him, even for a few hours while he slept. And, she realized with a huge smile of satisfaction, from now on they would never have to be apart again.

Cam stirred and saw her smiling at him. "What are you thinking about?"

"I'm thinking we need to get one of those credit cards with frequent flier miles."

"I'm thinking we should buy our own plane."

"Can we do that?" she asked.

"Not yet, but my agent assures me I'm about to make a substantial amount of money."

"Hmm," she said, tapping her lips with her index finger.

"What?"

"You gave me the motivation I need to get you enough money to buy something with leg room."

He grinned at her and held open his arms. "That's my Belle."

EPILOGUE

Two weeks later, Cam was still in New York. Somehow, he couldn't bring himself to leave Belle. Although they had promised to make time for each other, he was having his doubts about the logistics. Previously he had thought no one worked more than he did on the ranch. Now he knew better. Belle routinely put in eighteen-hour days, meeting up with Cam for a quick lunch or late supper. During her absence, he occupied himself by writing, a luxury he wasn't able to indulge in much during his time in Montana. However, writing about someone else falling in love was only making him miss Belle more. Something had to be done about their situation, and soon.

As he strolled through Central Park one afternoon, an idea suddenly occurred to him, causing him to stop short in the middle of a pathway. What if they got married now? So far they had been talking about taking things along the traditional route—dating long distance for a while until they became engaged and then splitting their time between locations after they were married.

But Cam could see too many potential problems with that scenario. They were going to get married eventually, and they both knew it. Why wait? Why not do it now and save the hassle of dating long distance? It was winter. Things on the ranch weren't exactly dead, but this was their slowest season. He could move to New York for the next few months and bring Belle back with him in the springtime for calving season.

He picked up the pace as he began walking again, smiling. Yes, this was the perfect plan. First things first, he needed an engagement ring. Normally Cam would have no idea how to go about such a thing, but even he had heard of Tiffany's. Surely if he threw enough money at them, they would tell him what to buy.

The store looked intimidating, and stepping inside, the feeling didn't go away. He swept off his Stetson and held it in his hands until he caught the eye of a friendly-looking salesperson. She directed him to the ring section and began explaining different cuts, sizes, and bands. Immediately Cam was overwhelmed, and out of his element. He had never touched a piece of jewelry, much less owned one. The woman, sensing his confusion, told him to simply look for something that reminded him of Belle.

With that thought in mind, Cam found the perfect ring after only a few minutes of looking. It was like Belle, one of a kind and high quality. It wasn't as flashy as some of the larger rocks, but he was certain she would approve.

Next he turned his attention to the proposal. Ideally he would take her to the park and pop the question on a carriage ride or somewhere equally romantic. But it was fall and, though New York had nothing on Montana, it was still cold. In the end, Cam decided to order room service in his hotel because he couldn't imagine getting down on one knee in a restaurant in front of a bunch of nosy gawkers. The thought of getting down on one knee reminded him he needed her father's permission. As soon as he left Tiffany's, he pulled out his phone and called Mr. Landry.

The Landrys were shocked, yet effusive. All they asked was that they be present for the wedding. Cam promised to fly them out on his dime, and the situation was settled. He headed back toward his hotel feeling a serene sense of accomplishment when he realized he hadn't made a date with Belle.

Knowing better than to trust Belle when it came to her schedule, he called her assistant, Ethan. Cam had at first been wary of Belle's assistant. How could someone spend so much time with his Belle and not fall in love with her? What if this Ethan person harbored a secret crush on her? But meeting Ethan had put his mind to rest. He wasn't prissy like Storm had been, but neither was he pining for Belle. He seemed to hold a sisterly affection for her, and that worked out fine for Cam. He considered himself a good judge of character, and he sensed Ethan was a nice guy, despite his fancy New York haircut.

Ethan assured him Belle's last meeting would be over by six o'clock that evening. Taking no chances, Cam asked him to write his name in the schedule so Belle would be sure to get home at a reasonable hour.

"I'll try," Ethan said, sounding amused. Cam thought he was having a really good time watching his boss with a man who was her equal. As far as he could tell, there weren't many people in Belle's life with enough nerve to stand up to her. "But you know Belle," Ethan continued. "Work has a way of consuming her."

"I know," Cam agreed. "Please tell her it's important."

He disconnected the call and went to arrange a special dinner at the hotel. For him, a special dinner consisted of steak and some form of potatoes, but he tried to think what Belle might like and ordered sushi for her.

At five, everything was arranged when, in a panic, he realized he needed candles for his candlelight dinner. He frantically searched his mind, trying to think of which store might carry candles in Manhattan, when it occurred to him that such a fancy hotel probably had candles on hand. Five minutes later the candles were arranged, and Cam sat back, thinking.

The scene was set. Now he needed the script, so he took out a piece of paper and began to write his proposal. By the time six o'clock rolled around, the food was ready, the candles were lit, the proposal was perfect, and there was no Belle.

He remained patient until seven.

By eight, he was fuming.

Calls to her office had yielded no response, but he knew she was there. He jammed his Stetson on his head and stormed out of the hotel. Usually he preferred to walk everywhere in New York, but this time he hailed a cab. He strode toward Belle's office, debated running up the fifty flights of stairs to burn off his anger, decided to save his anger, and took the elevator.

Belle was in a meeting room in the center of the agency. Her boss, Nancy, sat on one side while her assistant, Ethan sat on the other. It had been a harrowing day full of minor irritations that put her in a bad mood. Nothing had gone right today, which was why she wasn't surprised when Ethan looked up and said, "Uh-oh."

She didn't even look up to see what had caused the comment. And then she was being lifted into the air.

"I tried to tell her," Ethan said, holding up his hands in surrender. "I put it on her schedule and reminded her twice."

Cam nodded at him as he threw a protesting Belle over his shoulder. "Excuse us," Cam said. He had to say it loudly over Belle's howling disapproval. He carried her to her office, grabbed her coat and purse, and threw those over her before striding casually to the elevator. He kept hold of her, allowing the energy it took to carry her to burn off some of his anger, until some of what she was saying finally came through.

"I'm not done with work," Belle protested. "Are you crazy? You can't carry me out of my job."

They reached the outside of the building, and he finally set her down. "Yes, I am crazy. I must be; that's the only explanation." She stood openmouthed and sputtering as he spun on his heel and walked away.

"Wait," she called. Her heels clicked on the pavement as she trotted to catch up with him. When he didn't slow down, she jumped on his back, but he still didn't break stride. "Where are you going?"

"Home," he bit off.

"Home to your hotel, or home to Montana?"

"What do you care?" he growled.

"What do you mean what do I care? Can you wait a minute? I

cannot have a conversation on your back like a howler monkey. Just stop walking."

He stopped abruptly, causing her to jerk forward before sliding down his back and landing in an ungraceful puddle on the sidewalk. He turned, making no move to help her up. Somehow she hauled herself up, smoothing her hands down her skirt to make sure her underpants weren't showing. "Now what is going on? What is this about? I thought things were going well."

"I'm sure in your mind they were. You're doing exactly what you've always done, working yourself to death and seeing me whenever you can afford a minute. I've tried to fit myself into your mold, Belle, but I'm done. This isn't going to work if you're not willing to make concessions, and I can see you're not." He turned again and began walking away.

With an exasperated huff, she jogged to catch up with him again, grabbing his arm to halt him. "Stop. Why are you so angry with me today of all days?"

"I had Ethan put it on your schedule. You were done at six. You were supposed to come home."

"Something came up," she explained.

"Something always does. Something always will if you let it. And you always let it. You're not ready for this; you're not ready for me."

He turned and she tightened her grip on his arm. "Cam, so help me if you walk away again, I'm going to take off my stiletto and stab you with it. I work a lot; I get that. But I thought you understood going into this I'm driven."

"There's a fine line between being driven and being a workaholic, Belle. You've crossed it, and I have no faith you're willing to uncross it." He sighed wearily and shook his head. "I was going to ask you to marry me tonight. I had it all worked out perfectly. But then you didn't show up, and I started picturing more nights like this one. I don't want to live like this forever. I don't want to raise our kids alone. I don't want to be alone. I want to be with you."

"Marry you?" she whispered. "You were going to propose?"

He nodded.

She blinked at him a few times before bursting into tears.

His mouth fell as his heart twisted. Belle wasn't a crier, and the effect her tears had on him was profound. "Don't," he urged, moving closer so he could touch her. "Don't cry."

She pressed her face to his shirt and wept harder. "I'm sorry," she said between sobs. "I didn't mean to…I'm so used to…For so long, work has been my…Don't leave me."

He took her in his arms, sliding his hand gently up and down her spine. "I'm not leaving. Don't cry."

Her arms circled his neck, and she clung until her tears finally came to an end. Still, she shuddered pathetically with every other breath. "I can change," she promised.

"Can you, Belle?" He tipped her face up so he could look into her tear-drenched eyes. "We're both going to have to compromise, but so far I feel like I'm the only one who is doing the compromising."

"I will." She skimmed her mind, trying to work out a reasonable schedule he would approve of. "I can cut back to twelve hour days."

Cutting six hours out of her work day was huge, and Cam knew it. "What if you work four twelve hour days and one day you can work as long as you want to get caught up?" he suggested. "But no weekends. The weekends will be ours."

She nodded enthusiastically. "I can do that."

He smiled. She smiled.

"There's one more thing," he said.

"What?" she asked, her tone wary.

"You're going to marry me. This weekend."

"This weekend?" she croaked.

He nodded, let her go, pulled out the ring, and dropped to one knee on the cold sidewalk. He had completely forgotten the perfect proposal he memorized, but it didn't matter. "Belle, I love you. Will you marry me?"

She blinked at the dazzling ring, thinking it was perfect. Cam was perfect; everything was perfect. "One condition," she said, unable to resist a little bit of bargaining.

"What is it?" he asked.

"When your mom inevitably does a portrait of us or our children, please don't make me hang it in our living room."

He chortled a laugh. "We'll put it in my office with the wolves. Is that it? Because my knee has lost all feeling."

"That's it. Oh, and, yes, I'll marry you," she said.

He stood and swept her into his arms, bestowing her ring and a kiss at the same time, knowing for certain life with Belle Landry—soon to be King—would never be boring.

THANK you for reading *Cowboy Found,* the third book in the Kings of Montana Series. For more books, please check out my website at www.vanessagraybartal.com